ILLUSTRATIONS by ROBERT STOCKS

First published in Great Britain in 2020 by
Herbrand Press, Bernard Mansions, Herbrand Street,
Bloomsbury,
London WC1N 1LB

Text copyright© Robert Goodale 2020
Illustrations copyright© Robert Stocks 2020

ISBN: 978-0-244-57690-5

HOLLOWEEN is currently available to listen to on Google Play. However,
a few minor alterations to the text have occurred since it was recorded. The
version that is coming out on Audible will follow the text of this publication
much more accurately.

"The people and the pupils on this island come from a wide variety of religious faiths, backgrounds and beliefs. But we, at this school, do not pretend to have any answers. All we do know is that anyone who comes here is a Sagacitor. In other words, you have lived another life before this one."

— Head Teacher, Old Souls' School,
Old Souls' Island.

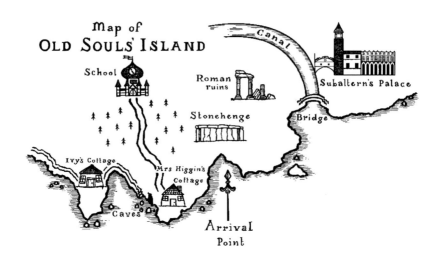

Map of
OLD SOULS' ISLAND

School

Roman ruins

Stonehenge

Canal

Subaltern's Palace

Bridge

Ivy's Cottage

Mrs Higgin's Cottage

Caves

Arrival Point

1. Notes and Queries

I love silence, don't you? Especially in the classroom. It's the only time that I can hear myself think. It's the only time that I can see things clearly in my mind.

I mean how are you supposed to be able to work out the values of x and y when Daryll's accusing you of stealing his rubber, Talisha's telling you about her cat hitting his head against the window last night and Tyrone's tapping his pencil and singing some rap song about how much he hates maths. That's three things too many going on in my head when all I want is one.

But the morning of November 28th wasn't like that. That particular morning, there was silence and it was far too precious, far too peaceful for anyone to want to break. Daryll had found his rubber, Talisha was daydreaming about her cat and I was on the verge of cracking the x + y sum that Jermaine had set me. Even Tyrone seemed to be happy, curled up around his desk, getting on with his sums and wallowing in the warmth and tranquillity of it all.

I would have gone on to say that this silence really was golden, had I not suddenly realised that I'd made a mistake in my working out which made all the rest of my calculations wrong – so completely and utterly wrong that I picked up my exercise book and threw it as hard as I could onto the floor.

'Do you want to have a cool down, Felix?' said Ms Bird, looking down at the book, which was now splayed out over the carpet.

For a moment, I wasn't going to answer, but then I took a couple of deep breaths and looked up.

'No, it's all right, miss. I think I'm OK now.'

'Good. Well, in that case,' said Ms Bird, realising that there was no point in carrying on with this particular session, 'we'll move on to Geometry. Tyrone and Talisha, would you give out the assessment books. Imran, if you could collect the work books…'

'Yes, miss.'

The noise level jumped from one to a hundred within seconds and order turned into disorder. I was still too annoyed with myself to join in though. So I opened up my assessment book, only to find a crumpled up piece of paper, smelling of stale lemon juice, with a handwritten message on it:

Please take this note when no one is looking, particularly your teacher, and put it into your pocket. You may read it at your leisure when you are in a private place, but you will have to hold it up to a light bulb first, as what follows is written in invisible ink.

2

I folded it in half, slipped it into my back pocket – while Ms Bird was busy changing the slides on the interactive whiteboard – and then put my hand up just as she turned round to address the class.

'Felix, it's my turn now. You can ask your questions afterwards.'

'Sorry, miss, but I…'

'You need to go out?'

'Yes.'

'So you **are**…'

'…Yes.'

'You do pick your moments, don't you. This means that you'll have missed all the instructions. All right. I can see…'

'Thank you, miss,' I said, heading for the door.

Although no one was in the corridor, the chances were that the head teacher would come round the corner at any moment. So I made a beeline for the toilets, took the note out of my pocket and held it up to a light bulb. As soon as the invisible ink had come through, I went straight into a cubicle, put the seat down, perched myself on top of it and started reading:

Hello. I have been asked to contact you as you have been selected to take part in a special activity which I can't, for reasons of security, tell you any more about at the moment. What I can do though is to ask you a question: Have you ever felt that you were born into the wrong time? By that I mean, do you sometimes think that you would have liked to have been alive during a different age of history? If you do, what I'm going to tell you about might well interest you.

If you would like to hear more, please tear off the smiley emoji at the bottom of this note and stick it onto the face of your Fitbit. If you're not interested, please put the sad face emoji there instead. Whatever your decision, please tear up the note itself as soon as you have read it.

We had been given so many warnings about not talking to strangers or responding to messages online, but this was not **online**. This was at school. So I could probably trust that part of it and then see what happened next. It was too intriguing just to dismiss. I thought that I might as well follow this up and at least see if it was genuine. If I was asked to do anything which felt in any way suspicious, I could then put a stop to the whole thing immediately and report it. For the moment however, I would keep this all to myself.

As I came back out into the corridor, I almost collided with Mrs Mensah, the head teacher.

'And what might you be doing out of class, Mr Featherstone?'

'I had one of my…'

She looked down at me, through her tortoise shell glasses, with one of those looks which made you realise that you didn't need to say anything else.

'Felix Featherstone, we have a contract with you. Not just a verbal one, but a written one, agreed by your class teacher, me, dad and lastly – but by no means leastly – you.'

'Yes, miss. I know.'

'I'm glad you do, Felix. So I won't have to remind you that the agreement states that if you have to leave the classroom, you stray no further than the corridor outside it. You have just made a mockery of that contract – and of all of us. Obviously we have been too lenient with you. When you go to upper school next year, they won't be anything like as sympathetic as we have been to your temper tantrums.'

I should probably explain that I was one of those annoying kids who got angry very easily and had to leave the classroom a lot. But wouldn't you if you kept getting the blame for just about everything that went wrong at home, including your mum's death. The stupid thing, though, was that *home* was the only

4

place where I didn't have any outbursts. That's probably because if I had, my dad would have had an even bigger one. And you didn't want to be around when that was happening.

'How old are you, Felix?'said Mrs Mensah, as I looked at her vacantly.

'I'm thirteen…in two days' time, miss.'

'Are you?' said Mrs Mensah, as if this had some kind of significance.

'Yes.'

'Felix, you are much loved at Larkfield and you have so much potential waiting to be tapped – if only you could break out of this endless cycle of…immaturity. Please try a bit harder this year.'

'I will, miss. Honest, miss. I'll try.'

'Get back to your classroom now,' she bellowed teasingly.

'Yes, miss.'

And that's when it all started – or at least that's when I thought it all had started. Now I look back on everything though, there were other things that happened before that – only I didn't realise they were happening at the time that they did, if you know what I mean.

The first was when I was on the tube on the way back from my grandpa's allotment. This old lady got out of her seat at Baker Street and she was having real difficulty picking up her shopping. So I asked if I could help and she was very grateful. I don't think she realised that it wasn't my stop though. Anyway, as we walked along the platform, she said to me, 'Well at least we don't have to sleep down here anymore.' And instead of asking her what she meant by that or telling her that World War Two was eighty years ago and she must have got a bit confused, I said, 'No. It can't have been very comfortable, although I always thought it looked rather cosy.' And she said, 'Yes, it was as a matter of fact – now you come to mention it. I take it that you never underwent that particular ordeal.' And I said, 'No. Not that particular one. But I remember watching it on the newsreels at the cinemas when it was happening.' Why on earth did I say that? I was almost telling her that I'd been around in the 1940s. What made it even weirder was that a week later I went to see the London Marathon with my grandpa. And there she was, not amongst the spectators but on the road, running – not that fast, but she was running alright.

The second thing was that on the night of Halloween that year, the new girl in our class, Edith, the one with the round face and blond hair tied up in a bob, came up to me and asked me if I was going to the party that night at school. I said that there was nothing I liked more than dressing up as the devil and scaring people, but it never really worked in our school hall, especially since the teachers insisted on keeping the fluorescent lighting on. She agreed and then said that if I liked proper Halloween, then I would really like HOLLOWEEN. When I asked her what that was, she said that she couldn't tell me, that it was a secret, that it was far too cool for school, but that I would definitely find out about it sometime.

And now there was this – a message in my exercise book. Had I ever wished that I had lived in another period of history? Definitely. Sometimes I hated how boring and grey everything was in my life. So the answer had to be 'YES'. On my way back to the classroom, I licked the back of the smiley emoji and stuck it onto my FitBit. It looked a bit odd, but I don't think that anyone noticed because I didn't get any comments. Although, come to think of it, someone must have done because later in the morning, I found another note – in my science book this time.

There was no point in going to the toilets at lunchtime to read it, as there would be too many people in there. That would have to wait until after school, unless I faked another temper tantrum during lessons. But then I would just be drawing attention to myself at a time when I needed to remain secretive. What was more important at this point was quizzing Tyrone, Talisha and

Imran. The only problem was that they'd all made a beeline for the cage, in order to make sure they got their football slot.

When we got out from school, I walked across the fields with Jermaine past the back of Wormwood Scrubs Prison.

'My dog's gone off this place,' said Jermaine. 'You have to tug on the lead to get him to walk around here. Even then, he refuses to move.'

'Probably worried that someone might capture him and put him in prison.'

'Yeah, that's probably it…Oh my god!' he suddenly went. 'They've spotted us.'

'Who?' I said.

'The guards! Quick! In the shrubbery!'

We rushed into the wooded area by the side of the path and I crouched down. Jermaine tried to do the same, but his frizzy hair got caught up in the branches.

'You see,' whispered Jermaine, looking up at the wall of the prison.

'See what?' I whispered back.

'They're just about to put the searchlight on us...'

'Oh, yeah,' I said, despite the fact that I really wasn't in the mood for all that sort of thing that evening.

'So, here's the plan. I'll give myself up and distract them, while you make a run for it.'

That prison took on a new identity on a daily basis, as did we. One day, we were in our F22s, dropping cluster bombs around a fortified city; the next, we were storming the Eternal Palace in Azeroth; and today, we were some dudes who'd just escaped from a prisoner of war camp.

'OK,' I said. 'Do I come back afterwards, though?'

'No, just keep on running. There's no turning back,' he said, as he rushed out into the open and then performed a slow motion sequence in which he was being shot in just about every part of his body. I, meanwhile, raced off along the footpath until I suddenly realised that I'd run straight past Tyrone.

'What's the hurry, Stonefeather?'

'Oh, nothing. Jermaine and I have just escaped from…' I said, as I came to a standstill and pointed up at the prison. 'He's just been shot, but I got away.'

'Oh, cool,' he said matter-of-factly.

'Um, Tyrone…Do you by any chance know about …'

'The Game? Yeah, of course.'

'Are you…er…playing it as well?'

'No. Apparently I don't qualify.'

'Don't you?'

'No, but the point is that you do.'

'Who's sending out the notes then?'

'Oh, a neighbour of mine.'

'What's his name?'

'Ah! That would be telling.'

'Is he to be trusted?' I said a bit anxiously.

'Yeah. I think so. He's not a cheat – if that's what you mean.'

'Well, sort of.'

'Yes, he'll play fair and square alright. What is this game you're playing exactly?'

'Ah, well. That would be telling,' I said, breaking back into a run again and heading back home.

As soon as the lift arrived at the fifteenth floor of Trevelyan Tower, I made a dash for my front door. I was so excited that I could hardly get the key in the lock. Once inside, I called out to check that no one was home.

'Dad!'

No answer. Excellent. I took the note out of my back pocket, turned on a standard lamp and allowed its magic to work.

Hello, again. Thanks for putting the smiley emoji on your watch. Now I can tell you what this is all about. You may not be

8

*aware of it, but there is a day in our calendar called Holloween. It's a bit like Halloween, only it's on the last day of November instead of the last day in October. Anyway, it's kind of the opposite of Halloween, but also very similar, if you get me. On Halloween, the wall between the earth and another dimension thins and all the spirits and ghosts come through just for that night and then return from whence they came as if nothing had happened. On Holloween, it's the other way round. It's us that go through the wall, or rather the **hollow** bit of atmosphere that opens up for several hours, not to where the ghosts are but to a magical island. But we don't terrify anyone there. In fact we are made to feel most welcome. I went last year and I wouldn't have missed it for...well...all the Haribos in the UK. By the way, you get brought back to Earth before daylight on December 1st.*

If you are interested in joining us, please send a note to me, Oliver Bailey (Year 8) at Fairview Secondary School, London W10 1BB and we'll come and collect you.

PS Even if you can get hold of my phone number, please do not text me or send me anything through social media. If you were to do that, it would be out there in the ether for good and one of the world's best kept secrets would be revealed for the first time for thousands of years. And we don't want to be the people responsible for that, do we!

There wasn't any time to lose. My dad would be back soon. I quickly googled Fairview Secondary School and saw all the pictures of the form captains, including Oliver. That all seemed OK. So I fished out an envelope and a bit of writing paper from the drawers and then wrote a note to say that I would love to come. Holloween parties were supposed to be so much cooler than Halloween. Also, it was on the same date as my birthday. I then hurriedly wrote the name and address on the envelope, stuck a stamp on it and went back out of the flat, putting the note inside as I went. It was only after I had posted the letter and arrived back on the fifteenth floor that I begun to have second thoughts. What had I signed up to? How could I reverse all of this? I could always ask Tyrone to pass a message on to Oliver to say that I'd changed my mind and didn't want to go on this trip after all. I wouldn't have minded if it was just a party, but travelling to another dimension was a different thing altogether – I thought, as I looked out over London, slumped back onto my bed and then fell into a trance.

2.   Cold Feet

When my dad came knocking on my door the next morning, I was dead relieved to find myself back in my own room. The long, drawn out dream that I'd been having had taken me to a Victorian classroom, where the teacher kept putting a dunce's hat on my head and making me stand in the corner – which everyone else thought was hilarious.

As I got dressed for school, it suddenly dawned on me what I'd signed up for – when I'd sent off that note. That wasn't a dream. It was real and I had no idea where that was going to take me to.

'Felix, your breakfast's ready,' my dad called out through the door.

'Coming,' I shouted back.

'I've done a fry up. So be quick – or it'll be overcooked.'

'OK.'

Eating my breakfast was unimportant though – in comparison to what else needed to be done before going to school. If I sent another note off to Oliver Bailey, I could perhaps stop this weird other-dimension stuff from happening. I sneaked into the living room and pulled out some paper and an envelope from the drawer.

'Felix!'

'Yes, Dad.'

'Your breakfast will be ruined.'

'Coming.'

'What are you doing in the living room?'

'Oh, I just needed to get something.'

'Come and have your breakfast first.'

'OK,' I said as I hastily scribbled a note.

'I said...'

'Yes, Dad,' I said, sticking a stamp on the envelope, looking up the postal code of Fairview Secondary School on the computer and then going into the kitchen.

'Don't say I don't try and look after you. Here you are,' said Dad, as he presented me with dried up bacon, rubberised egg, that you could throw against the wall and catch, and shrivelled mushrooms – just like my great grandma's fingers used to look.

'Oh. Thanks, Dad,' I said, looking with horror at what had been placed in front of me.

'This is all because you didn't come when I called you,' he said, wiping the grease from his tattooed arm and then running it through his already slicked-down hair. 'What were you doing in the living room?'

'Just getting something for school.'

'What?'

'Oh, nothing important.'

'So nothing important takes priority over my cooked breakfast, does it? You're doing this deliberately. Just because there's only one of me. If your mum were still alive, she'd be doing the cooking and I'd be dragging you by the ear into the kitchen. It's bad enough that I have to cook and clean for you, let alone go out and earn us the daily crust. But you dawdling around on top of all that really does take the biscuit. Now sit down and eat it up. All of it.'

'I'm not being rude or nothing, but the egg will make me throw up.'

'Just make sure you do that in the toilet then.'

'My teeth aren't strong enough for...'

'For what?'

'Nothing, Dad.'

Bits of rubbery egg were sticking to the side of my teeth and the hard sharp shards of bacon cut into my gums and the side of my mouth.

'Big anniversary tomorrow.'

'What do you mean?' I said with difficulty.

'Ten years since your mum passed away.'

'Yes, I know.'

'Well, why did you ask what I meant then?'

'I thought you meant...'

'Meant what?'

'Nothing, Dad,' I said quickly, not wanting to bring up my controversial birthday.

'You're going to your grandpa's for tea this evening,' said Dad as a matter of fact.

'Oh. OK.'

'Yeah, I've got some meetings to go to.'

Down the pub, I thought. It was always the same, every year – the lead up to my birthday or rather the anniversary of my mum's death. November 30th was not a day to be celebrated. In fact, it was quite the opposite.

'Anyways, I'll probably be back late tonight. So I'll see you tomorrow, Son.'

13

'Yes, see you tomorrow.'

As I wandered off to school, I wondered whether my birthday tomorrow would be as terrible as it normally was. Was this the way that it was always going to be or would my dad eventually let go of the past and start living in the present? After I'd posted the note to Oliver Bailey, I felt a bit better though. At least I wouldn't have to be travelling to some other dimension in 36 hours time.

School was really boring that day. Jermaine was in football mode at break and lunchtime, which meant that I didn't really have anyone to hang out with. I wanted to talk to Tyrone though and tell him that I'd got cold feet about 'playing the game' and ask him if he could knock on Oliver's door the next day and make sure that he had got the second note. However, every time I approached him, he was otherwise engaged. Edith, on the other hand, seemed insistent on talking to me though.

'Heard about Holloween yet?' she said, looking at me intensely with her bright green eyes.

'Yeah, I have as a matter of fact,' I said reluctantly.

'Going to any parties?' she said, giving me a little wink.

'Well, I have been invited.'

'I told you. So you are going?'

'Um…not sure.'

'They're really good. I promise you. There's no way I'd say that if they weren't.'

'No, I know,' I said, just as Tyrone ran past.

'Um…Tyrone!'

'Yeah, Stonefeather.'

'Will you see...?'

'Can't talk now, bruv. Places to go. People to see, man.'

#

14

I loved my grandpa. We'd talk about things that no one else would, except for Jermaine. We'd watch old black and white movies together and immitate the ridiculous accents that people used to have then. We'd talk in gobbledygook and he'd do the best bad-grandad dancing that I've ever seen. So it was always great to see him, even though he was ill. The chicken salad wasn't up to much, but the company was.

'Grandpa.'

'Yes, Felix.'

'Do you think that there's really such a thing as another dimension?'

'What, like in science fiction books, you mean?' he said, gently stroking his grey stubble with the back of his fingers.

'Yes.'

'Well, I don't know. Brian Cox seems to think that there is. He may well be right.'

'Do you think that humans can get there?'

'Oh, no. Not in this day and age. Not unless you die, that is.'

'Die!' I said, a bit alarmed. 'Is that how all those spirits and ghosts can get to us on Halloween? Because they're dead.'

'Yes, I suppose it is…if you really…'

'So, if they can get to us, we must be able to get to them. But we'd have to die first.'

'I suppose so.'

This was really beginning to worry me. No one had said anything about having to die in order to get to another dimension on Holloween.

'Do you think that Grandma and my mum both went to another dimension.'

'Yes, but I've no idea where that is or what it is. I do know that they're happy though.'

'How do you know?'

'This tells me,' he said pointing to his stomach.

'What? Your belly button?'

'No. The gut, silly!'

'Did my mum really not like me?'

'What are you talking about, boy. She loved you more than she ever loved anything.'

'But I was a difficult child, wasn't I?'

'No more than any other two-year-old.'

'But that's what killed her, wasn't it?'

'What?' said Grandpa incredulously.

'My being difficult.'

'What makes you think that?'

'Oh. Nothing really,' I said, not wanting to dwell on this.

'Is that what your dad's been…?'

'No, not exactly.'

'No. Your mum had cancer and it had spread. That's what killed her. Same as I've got.'

There was nothing I could say to that. I couldn't bear to think that my grandpa might die soon and the droplets that were coming out of my eyes made me realise that it was time to go. All this talk about dying in order to get to another dimension didn't help either. When I took the lift up from the ground floor – where my grandpa's flat was – to the fifteenth, I was desperately hoping that my dad wouldn't be back. But he was. And so was his girlfriend.

'Oh, I was wondering what time you'd be back. Nice tea?'

'Yes, it was great,' I said, despite the fact that it wasn't really and that I'd got all depressed.

'This is Suzy, by the way. You might see more of her in the days to come.'

'Pleased to meet you, Felix,' she said coldly.

'How do you do,' I said.

'Oh, very well – since you ask. Isn't it past your bedtime?'

'Yes, it is.'

'Well, off you go then.'

'Goodnight,' I said, but there was no response other than the stifled giggles that I could hear after I'd closed the door behind me.

3. Holloween

November the thirtieth was quite an anxious day for me, wondering whether Oliver had got the second note or not, whether I still might be expected to go to this party and whether someone might turn up at the door to collect me. I kept myself to myself and avoided Edith at all costs. I wasn't going to let her talk me into doing something I didn't want to do. When Miss Bird let our maths class go at home time, she asked me if I could stay behind for a moment.

'Everything all right, Felix?'

'Yes, miss.'

'It's just that you've seemed a bit…Is it because it's your…?'

Miss Bird knew all about my birthday.

'Oh no, miss. It's just that I didn't sleep very well last night. Sorry.'

At least the last bit was true.

'Don't be sorry, Felix. I just wanted to check that you were OK. Maybe you should get an early night tonight.'

'That's a good idea. I will,' I said, suddenly inspired.

'And then we'll see you nice and refreshed tomorrow,' she said. Little did she realise what might be in store for me.

'I hope so. I'll see you tomorrow, miss.'

'See ya tamarra, Felix,' she said in that really corny American accent she puts on sometimes.

'Bye, miss.'

That was a really good idea of hers. I could go to bed early and tell Dad that I wasn't feeling very well. That way I wouldn't have to talk to him that evening or pretend to celebrate my birthday with a bowl of birthday cake ice cream. It wasn't like I ever got anything from him, not even a card.

As usual, my dad wasn't back from work when I returned to the flat. I got straight into my pyjamas, grabbed a snack and a cup of tea from the kitchen and then went to bed. If someone did come to collect me to go to the Holloween party before Dad got back, I could just not answer the door. If, on the other hand, my dad was in, I could let him deal with it. They'd soon get the message. By nine o'clock, there was still no sign of my dad and I allowed my head to drop onto the pillow, falling into a deep and dream filled sleep.

One of these dreams or nightmares, the one in which Jermaine and I had crash landed our F-22 aircraft into the sea, was interrupted. As I came to, I suddenly realised that it was not the waves that were throwing me up into the air but someone who was in my room, who had lifted me out of bed.

'Oh my god! Who the hell are you? What are you doing? Get out of my room now or I'll call the police.'

'Oh, I'm sorry,' said the boy with neat hair and spectacles, 'I didn't mean to wake you. I thought that you were expecting me though.'

'What do you mean? What's happening? Who are you? How did you get into my room?'

'Well, to answer all your questions in the order you asked them: firstly, you are being 'collected'; secondly, I am your collector; and thirdly, I have arrived here through the window that is currently open between The Island and here on this auspicious night.'

'But I sent a note to say that I didn't want to go to the party after all.'

'Which party?'

'The Holloween party.'

'Oh, no. It's not a party. It's a whole way of life.'

'For who?'

'For Sagacitors.'

'Who?'

'Sagacitors in the making. Like us.'

'What do you mean – Sagacitors? I'm not a Sagacitor, or even one that's in the making, for that matter. I don't even know what one is.'

'Oh, I think you are – without even knowing it.'

'How come?'

'Well, one qualification is your soul.'

'What about it?'

'It's had some previous existences. You have lived other lives before this one.'

'Have I?'

'Yes.'

'Are you telling me that I've got an old soul?'

'I'm telling you that you are an old soul and that I have come to take you to Old Souls' Island.'

'Do I have to die in order to go there?' I said.

'No, of course not.'

'Well, even so, I don't want to go.'

'Oh, that is a pity.'

'Is it?'

'Yes, they're very keen to have you there.'

'Are they?'

'Very. Don't ask me why. I just know that there's something about you that's a bit more...how should I put it...special than your everyday old soul.'

'Are you serious?'

'Completely.'

'Well, I still don't want to go.'

'Very well. I can't force you. In fact, we have a strict policy of ensuring that all participants come completely of their own free will. I bid you good day then or rather goodnight.'

'Where will you go now?'

'Oh, back to Old Souls'. It doesn't take long. Or I might just hang around outside and try again in an hour's time.'

'But I'll be asleep by then.'

'I won't wake you up. I promise. However, if you do change your mind...and we would love it if you did...perhaps you could stay awake and we'll have another conversation then.'

'Well, I won't be awake,' I insisted.

'I'm sorry to hear that. But, as I said, I would never take anyone unwillingly. It's been a real pleasure to meet you, Felix,' he said and disappeared into the ether.

Now I was terrified. If I stayed awake, I might be persuaded to go. If I fell asleep, I might still be taken. How did I know that I could trust this person that could just come and go through my bedroom walls as he pleased. There was only one thing for it. I'd go down to Grandpa's and stay the night there.

I put on my dressing gown, got into my bedroom slippers, stuck my head round the door to make absolutely certain that Dad wasn't back and then sneaked out of the front door and into the lift.

Grandpa could tell that something was up and he tried to get it out of me what it was. There was no way that I was going to worry him with trips to other dimensions, so I started telling him about how horrible Dad was being.

'Did you ever have problems with any of your...um...family,' I said.

'Yes. Your grandma. She would boss me around like nobody's business. And then one day, I turned round to her and I said: "If you don't stop criticising me for everything I do, I'm off. I'm out of here." And I meant it.'

'And what happened?' I asked, but Grandpa, suddenly overcome with a coughing fit, was unable to answer.

'What happened?' I repeated.

'She stopped. I wish this blooming cough would stop,' he said but was again unable to continue – as the blooming cough was not going to stop. 'We never had another argument from that day until the day she died. You can't say that to your dad though.'

'I could. I could come and live with you, Grandpa.'

'I wish you could, but I'm not long for this world. That old cancer's eating me up by the day – as you can see. I might not even be here tomorrow morning.'

'Please don't say that.'

'But the one thing you can do, Felix, is stop being a victim. I just wish there was something that I could do for you before I go the way of all flesh. Take you on holiday or something. But I can't. You need to get away from it all. From your dad, his girlfriends, school.'

'Yes, maybe I do. Thanks, Grandpa,' I said and headed for the door.

'Where are you going?'

'Back to the flat. To my room.'

'You're not staying over then?'

'No. I'll be fine...at home.'

'You do as you please.'

'I...love...I...love coming here, Grandpa.'

'And I love seeing you, you little munchkin. Now get yourself to bed,' he said, as he got out of his chair.

'I will.'

'I need to get to bed myself. Suddenly come over all funny.'

'Thanks for the F-22 by the way. I can't wait to build it.'

'Sweet dreams.'

'And you, Grandpa. Night, night,' I said as I shut the front door and made my way back to the flat, thinking about what he had just said. There were ways of changing things. And at this moment in time, there was definitely something I could do – as long as I was brave enough.

As the lift doors started to close, someone called out to me.

'Happy Holloween, Felix.'

It was that woman – the one I'd helped with her shopping and then seen running in the London Marathon. What was she doing in the building? She lived in Baker Street. And how did she know about Holloween?

'And where have you been?' called out Dad, as I came through the front door.

'Oh, I didn't think that you were going to come back.'

'What do you take me for? That's enough of your insolence, you little…'

'Oh, no. I didn't mean it like that. It's just that I got frightened. So I went down to Grandpa's.'

'Frightened?' interrupted Suzy. 'How old is that boy of yours?'

'Twelve…No, thirteen – today. Happy Birthday, Son. I put a card in your room.'

'Thanks, Dad,' I said – a bit surprised.

'He'll need to toughen himself up now he's a teenager,' said Suzy. 'First time I've ever heard a teenager saying he's frightened.'

'I'd say. Anyway, you're back. And it's way past your bedtime. Off you go.'

'Yes, Dad.'

'I'll see you tomorrow then.'

'Yes, Dad.'

That did it. How dare that woman speak about me as if I was some kind of wimp. Under normal circumstances, that would have made me angry. But right now, it just made me even more determined to go to Old Souls' Land. There was no turning back now, that was for sure.

4. Old Souls' Land

As there was only half an hour to go before the collector returned, I had a quick look at Dad's birthday card, which had a picture of a cake with candles on. Was that his idea of a joke? Why didn't he just give me the real thing for once? I then turned off the light and just waited.

After about five minutes, I heard my dad and Suzy going out through the front door. Strange. The pubs would be closed by now. Then, at 23.46 precisely, I suddenly felt a presence in the room.

'Hello,' I whispered, thinking this must be that collector dude again.

There was no response but the presence remained. It felt warm and friendly. So I wasn't worried.

At 23.58 precisely, the collector, true to his promise, appeared like a hologram next to my wardrobe.

'Hello again,' I said.

'Hello,' the boy whispered back.

'Was it you that came ten minutes ago?'

'No.'

'You didn't send something ahead of you...or anything?'

'No.'

'Oh. Don't worry...OK. Let's do it then.' I said.

'Are you sure?'

'I couldn't be more certain.'

'Great. I'm Adrian by the way.'

'Hi, Adrian.'

'I do first need to remove some of the positive energy from the room though,' he said, pulling a number of spinning tops out of his rucksack, placing them around the room and setting them into motion. Apparently, they helped to bring out the negative energy in the atmosphere, which was what was needed to open up a point of entry to this other world. They were forged out of a special metal called planium, which you could only get in Old Souls' Land.

'So, Felix, if you just relax and let me carry you to the corner of the room.'

'Why the corner of the room?'

'Because that's where our portal appears to be,' he said, gathering up the tops. 'Now, if you let me pick you up. And if you can keep as still as possible.'

'OK. How long for?'

'Just a minute!'

'A minute?'

'No, sorry. I was trying to say: "Just a minute, I need to concentrate." But since you ask, it is indeed just about a minute. Ready?'

'Ready.'

'You might feel a bit sleepy. That's quite normal. It's me that has to stay sharp and concentrated.'

'OK.'

SLEEPY! How could I possibly feel sleepy when my whole body felt like it had been laid out on an operating table with doctors and nurses at either end, pulling my arms and legs so tightly that all my limbs felt like they were eight-foot long. Within seconds however, I was out for the count.

'OK. You can wake up now,' said the boy, as I found myself crawling out of the sea onto a rocky shore.

'Is this Old Souls' Land?' I said, marvelling at the place I'd just arrived at.

'It certainly is.'

'It looks a bit like a place I went on holiday to once.'

'Where was that?'

'Cornwall.'

As I begun to get my bearings, I could see that it was actually even more amazing than that. The rugged coastline and the crystal clear water were the same, but up above me was this weird looking landscape, full of exotic plants, trees, flowers and anything else that grew up from the ground. It was like they were all in a beauty contest, trying to compete with each other to be the one that everyone looked at.

'But the wildlife is more extraordinary than it is there,' I said, as I was taking it all in.

'Yes. It's all evolved here in its own rather peculiar way.'

'What, like that king-sized dragonfly?' I said, pointing up at an insect with multi-coloured scales. 'We don't have ones like that back home.'

'Nor here very often, actually. I've never seen one of those before. I think they're quite rare. Looks like it's been designed by Damian Hurst.'

'Oh, yeah. It's really amazing.'

'It certainly wants to draw attention to itself. And it seems to have taken a liking to you.'

'Yeah, it does,' I said, as the thing kept flying towards me in a continuous loop the loop.

'Yes, it's dancing around all over the place.'

'So, it's daytime here at the moment?' I said, suddenly realising that I'd moved from darkness to light in a few seconds.

'Yes. Look at your watch.'

I did. It was two o'clock in the afternoon. It was the only bit of modern technology that worked on this island – I was soon to discover. And that was only because it had made the correction as it broke through the wall between the two worlds. It would have recognised the fact that that was what it was doing and adjusted itself as it was happening. There was nothing to guide it here though. No satellites or anything.

'Aren't I supposed to be back home in six hours time?' I said.

'Yes, but that's not for ages.'

'Well, six hours.'

'Yes, but you do know that every minute on Earth is a day on Old Souls' Island.'

'What?'

'So you'll actually be away for…'

'360 days, which is nearly a year. A year!' I screamed. What on earth had I done? No one said anything about a year.

'Please, Felix. Calm down. I'll explain. It should have been on your note. You stay here for a year and return at five past six, just before the wall hardens up again. Then everything goes into reverse. Every minute here for a period of approximately six hours and five minutes is a day on Earth. That's why everything has to be timed so precisely.'

'So, in other words, the two worlds get back in sync with each other.'

'That's right,' said Adrian. 'Anyway, we better go and introduce you to Mrs Wiggins. She'll be wondering where we've got to. We're the last to arrive, you see.'

'OK. OK,' I said, trying to take this all in. 'A YEAR!'

'Yes. And that's where your home will be for A YEAR,' said Adrian, pointing along the cliff to a large, old, rambling cottage, covered in climbing plants.

'If you say so.'

'I do. Race you then?'

'All right. On your marks, get set…GO!' I said and got off to a flying start, shouting 'A YEAR!' all the way. As I approached the cottage, I took a quick look round to see my friend lagging behind, promptly tripped over a branch in the ground and fell flat on my face – directly in front of my landlady. I looked up to see a very proper and upright woman, with her hair neatly tied up in a bun.

'You must be Felix Featherstone,' she said, over-enunciating every word. She had one of those accents that seemed like it might have started off as cockney but ended up more like the Queen's.

'How did you know that?' I said, as I got myself up off the ground.

'Because your colleagues are here already,' she continued, ignoring my mishap. She must have seen it all before. 'I've put you into the Sea View room. Your fellow occupants thought that you'd appreciate it more than they would.'

'That is very kind of you, Mrs Wiggins.'

'Higgins.'

'I'm sorry?'

'The name is Higgins, with a 'haitch', not Wiggins. Goodness gracious.'

I could see that my new friend was trying to hide a grin.

'Anyway, it's not me that you should be thanking. It's these people.'

'Jermaine!' I said in disbelief as he suddenly appeared from behind the door. 'I don't believe it. Why on earth didn't you tell me you were coming?'

'Why didn't I tell you? What you chatting about, bruv? You know what the score was,' said Jermaine.

'Yes, we weren't supposed to tell anyone,' said Edith as she appeared too.

'And Edith as well! Ah. Now that's why you kept going on about Holloween. How did you know that I was a Sagacitor?' I said, trying to fathom it all out.

'Oh, I knew. I can always tell an old soul from a new one,' said Edith.

'How can you tell?'

'Oh. An old soul just looks like they've got a bit more wisdom and a bit more understanding of what's really going on.'

'I see. Is anyone else from school an old soul?'

'Yes. Layla, in year 7, but she shares a room with her sister. So the collectors wouldn't have been able to get her unnoticed.'

'Well, I'd better show you to your room, Master Felix,' said Mrs Higgins, who was beginning to feel left out.

'Master Felix? Is this Dickens' Land or something?'

'No, but some of us more…how should I put it…more mature people here have decided to identify with a former life. I used to run a very respectable boarding house in my last existence. Rooms to let and that sort of thing. I ran a very tight ship and my lodgers were all very respectful. Not like the ones you get in this day and age. You can live in the past here. That's one of the reasons people stay on. Can't do that back in TWAWKI.'

'TWAWKI?'

'Yes. The World As We Knew It.'

'Could you go back to TWAWKI if you wanted to?'

'In theory, yes. But I probably wouldn't know anybody and it would give my relations the most terrible shock. They must have thought that I'd departed from this very dear life of ours – years ago.'

'How old would you be?'

'The same as I am now: seventy-five. Now a word of warning to you all from one who has been here for fifty years. This island is an idyllic place and it does a very good job of training up Sagacitors. However, just occasionally, we get a bad apple, a malevolent old soul that tries to alter the way things are.'

'Is that happening at the moment then?' said Jermaine.

'I'm not saying that it is and I'm not saying that it isn't. Only Mrs Butcher told me the other day that she'd walked past the barometer and that it was bright pink, but her husband said that it was just her spooky imagination.'

'What barometer?'

'We have our own version of Stonehenge here and it acts as a barometer. If it stays its normal colour, it means that the energy on the island is good. If it changes colour and starts to go red however, we know that evil forces are at play. But anyway, we can't stand here chatting all day. We need to get you in readiness for school tomorrow.'

'School?'

'Yes, school.'

5. School

School was this massive Victorian church hall about half a mile's walk from the cottage down a footpath. It was actually more like a tunnel that had been carved out through some woodland. Its trees, or whatever they were, seemed to move and twitch as you passed them, even on a calm and windless morning like the one it was when Edith, Jermaine and I headed off the next day. I was feeling that exact same nervous anxiety that I'd had just over a year ago, when I was about to start at Larkfield. What would the other kids be like? Would I fit in? Would all the teachers be horrible?

Because no one was talking, I could take everything in, like our new uniforms, which weren't really new – or uniform for that matter. They were all a bit ragged and grey. Actually, they looked quite cool against the cartoon-like colours of the natural world around us.

The gigantic doors, more like gates, of the hall were open as we arrived and my collector friend was standing outside, taking photographs of everyone with a 1950s camera, made out of black plastic – just like the one my grandpa had on a shelf in his living room.

'Good morning. Good morning,' he said in between snaps. 'Get yourself a space in there if you can find one. You may have to do a bit of gentle nudging.'

The hall had a stage at one end with a staircase beside it, leading up to a gallery which ran all the way round the side of it. There were twenty-four doors leading off it. The walls of the hall were made out of wooden panels with all these statues of old souls who had spent time on the island. Some of them were quite famous.

The place was packed with roughly three hundred children, all about our age and wearing different variations of the ragged and grey look. Some were chatting away merrily, whilst others looked lost and isolated. I was so lucky to have my friends with me.

Suddenly, all of the doors up above opened in unison and twenty-four members of staff came out. One of them, who looked about sixteen, came down the staircase while the rest of them, who covered a variety of ages, looked on from up above. We were all immediately silent as the young dude – who had a clean-cut, fresh-faced look – came down onto the stage and started talking to us.

'I would just like to say how blissfully happy I am this morning, not only to greet all of you fledgling Sagacitors – or Springers, as you'll be called from now on – but also to have the honour of being your head teacher. Now, a couple of things that need to be pointed out. Firstly, I would like to assure you that your education here will have nothing whatsoever to do with

33

what you do at school at home. You will not, as I hope you all realise, be missing out on anything from there, not even a day – although you might find yourselves a bit tired and uncomfortable on the morning of your return. I should also warn you that, even though this won't be happening for another year, your TWAWKI clothes will no longer fit you properly and you won't have had much more than a couple of hours sleep. Secondly, I should say that we do not profess to know anything about science or religion here at Old Souls'. Of course, we all have our ideas, philosophies and opinions. But none of us know for sure how, for instance, this dimension connects with the Earth on Holloween. We also do not subscribe to any particular religion as we do not know for certain what happens to us when we stop being reborn – in other words when we die for good. What we **do** know though is what our past lives were. Now, before we do anything else, we need to get started on your identification processes. Your guides will call you individually for your first session. I should make it clear, before they do though, that although they need to find out who you were, the school's policy is that they do not reveal who they were. This merely gets in the way. Very good. May the morning commence!'

And then suddenly, people's names were being called from up above.

'Felix Featherstone! Room 21, please!'

As I followed my fellow pupils up the staircase, I was trying to figure out what it was that made old souls different to everybody else. They didn't look any older, but they did all seem to have something about them. Maybe just a bit of wisdom beyond their years – as Edith had said.

Looking in through the doors on the balcony, I could see that some of the guides were more distinctive – and stranger – than the children though. The door of Room 21, however, was closed. So I had to knock.

'Come in!'

I opened the door to find a young woman in a wheelchair, not the man who had called out my name. She appeared to be looking up at the ceiling.

'Hello, Felix.'

'Hi.'

'My name is Asha and I am going to be your guide – for today, anyway. Have you settled into Old Souls' yet or are you still suffering from 'first day-itis'?'

'No, I've settled in.'

'We need the truth, Felix.'

'What do you mean?'

'I mean that here at Old Souls', if we are to make any progress, we need to know what you are really thinking and what you are really feeling as well. Don't worry. You're not alone. Everyone has that problem when they first arrive. Where you come from, you almost have to tell white lies in order to survive.'

'Yes, you do.'

'At least you are aware of it.'

'Well, I wouldn't be here if I'd told the truth back at home.'

'No, you wouldn't, because your dad and your school would have prevented your journey from happening if they'd known. Here, however, if you tell lies…By the way, how do you think I look?'

'How do I think you look?'

'Yes. Am I pretty? Am I ugly?'

'Oh, you're…'

'Good. You're finding it difficult.'

'Yes.'

'Yes, because for the first time in your life, you have to be totally truthful. You can't just say "Oh, you're very beautiful", because I'm not.'

'Well you are, actually,' I said without any hesitation.

'You're very kind and I do believe you, even though I have no idea whether you're right...'

'Because you can't see.'

'I can't, nor never have been able to – in this life. However, I can remember what things looked like from all my other lives.'

'What were they?' I asked.

'In my most recent one, I was an explorer.'

'What sort?'

'I was on the first expedition to conquer Mount Everest.'

'In 1953?' I said, surprising even myself at how confident I was about the date.

'Yes, in 1953. I couldn't do that now, of course. The two most vital resources that I would need have been taken away from me – mobility and sight. Deliberately, I believe. I was a man of action. Now my greatest attribute is the power of perception. Anyway, I was, like I am here, a guide – on that expedition.'

What was weird was that I was beginning to get drawn in by all this. Although I didn't know anything about all this, it suddenly felt as though I knew **everything** about it and I started to tell her how grateful I was for her help on that expedition. I wouldn't have become a hero if it hadn't been for her. She had allowed me to be the one that got to the top first.

'Think nothing of it,' said Asha modestly.

'Just a moment, I was told that the guides don't normally reveal who they were in past lives.'

'We don't.' said Asha, with a smile.

'But you just have.'

'Have I, Felix? Or should I call you Edmund? We are also not required to tell the truth.'

'But we are!'

'Yes, of course you are. Otherwise, how on earth are we ever going to find out who you **were**. Let's leave it there for today though. Good, I thought that I was right about you. Thank you, Felix. That will do for today.'

As I went down the staircase, I peered down to see if I could spot Jermaine but got distracted by something annoying buzzing round my head, which I tried to swipe away. When I looked at it properly though, I suddenly realised that it was the dragonfly with multi-coloured scales that I'd seen when I arrived – or at least one of that species.

'Oh, my god! Sorry.'

The insect did a somersault in acknowledgement, flew towards the staircase and then went back to its hovering.

'What's it doing?' I said to myself.

'I think that it might want you to follow it,' called out Edith, who had been watching all of this unfold.

'Really?'

'Yes. See what happens if you do.'

'OK.'

I did just that and then it automatically flew a few more feet further forward.

'No, it's flying away again.'

'Well, keep following it then,' called out Edith.

I did as she suggested and walked up behind it as it flew up the stairs and along the corridor, until it had come to a stop again outside Room 16.

'OK. Keep going. I've caught up with you.'

The insect didn't keep going though. Instead of hovering this time, it flew round in a continuous halo-like circle above my head, giving me a bit more distance this time. I couldn't work this out. Did someone want to see me for another session? Surely they would have called down to me. I moved away from where I was to see if the insect would follow. It didn't but instead continued to circle above the exact same spot in front of Room 16. Obviously that's where I was supposed to be. So I went back and stood there, wondering what on earth this could all be about. Then suddenly, I overheard one of the guides talking to a fellow pupil.

'Can you not feel it? Do you not remember any of this?' said the guide.

'No, I don't. None of it,' said a voice that sounded like Jermaine's.

'This is very common, Jermaine. People who are told that they have attempted to kill someone in their last life are often in denial. In other words, they do not let themselves acknowledge the truth. And, of course, when it's happened in both of your previous lives, it's even harder to accept.'

'Are you saying that I might try to do it again in this life?'

'Quite possibly.'

'That's bad.'

'Yes, but we will do everything we can here to help you. It's a bit like being addicted to something though. Whereas most people just wouldn't do it, you have to spend your whole life stopping yourself from doing it.'

The insect headed off towards the staircase and I took this as my cue to make myself scarce.

So I was a hero in my previous life, while my best friend had been a murderer. This didn't make any sense. Jermaine was the kindest, gentlest and most sensitive person that I had ever met. If anyone was to have committed a brutal act, it would have been me. I found it so difficult to keep a grip on my anger at times that I could imagine myself losing control and doing something that I regretted. But then that was not the same as murder.

6. Lost Souls

The next day, I left early for school with Edith. I wanted to avoid seeing Jermaine and having to pretend that I didn't know anything about his one-to-one session.

'Find out anything interesting last night?' she said.

'What do you mean?'

'That dragonfly seemed particularly eager to show you something.'

'But it was just a dragonfly.'

'Nothing's just **anything** on Old Souls' Island.'

'How do you know so much about this place? Have you been here before or something?' I said, flippantly.

She looked at me hesitantly and then revealed that she had, insisting that I didn't let on about it to anyone. I should have realised before. It was pretty obvious now that I came to think of it. All that stuff about Holloween. In fact she seemed to know everything about everything and proceeded to tell me all about Sagacitors and how their purpose in life was to keep the Earth in check. Our job was to ensure that good always won out over evil. Without our influence, Earth would be doomed. And that was why we were there at that school. To learn how to encourage goodness amongst mankind without anyone realising that we were doing it.

'Incidentally, you don't know an old woman who lives near Baker Street tube station, do you?' I said, almost positive that she'd have an answer to that as well.

'What, Mrs Herbert? Yes, she's one of the scouts who go looking for Sagacitors. She spotted you, me and Jermaine.'

'Is everyone here a Sagacitor?'

'Yes, unless their previous life was a bad one. If that was the case, they wouldn't be suitable for the job. In fact, quite the opposite.'

'How can an old soul be bad?'

'Oh, it happens. They can be more evil than the good ones can be good.'

'Oh,' I said, determined not to tell her anything about Jermaine. Fortunately, a creature suddenly appeared on the pathway in front of us at that moment and we were both distracted.

'Oh, look. It's a fox.'

'Yes, although they call them orkins here,' said Edith as the animal froze for a second, had a good stare at us and then ran off. As it did so, something which looked like a badger, but with longer legs and longer ears, crawled immediately out in front of us.

'Well, this one's not nervous. Does it want us to stroke it?' I said.

'That's what it looks like, but be careful.'

'Why? It's not baring its teeth or hissing at us or anything.'

I bent down to stroke it and it then rolled over and allowed me to tickle its tummy.

'There you are…Ow!'

The horrible creature had suddenly turned on me and bitten my hand, just at the moment when Jermaine came running up the hill to catch up with us.

'What happened, man?' he said.

'I've been tricked. This cuddly-looking creature was asking me to stroke it and then it just bit me. What are they called, Edith?'

'That must have been a Janus-facer.'

'You have to be really careful who or what you trust in this world, it seems.'

'Yes, you do,' said Jermaine, not realising that I would know quite how meaningful what he had just said was. 'Do you want me to borrow you my handkerchief?'

'No, it's all right. I'll get it bandaged up at school. Those Janus-facers are the worst!' I said, trying to shift my attention away from what I now knew about Jermaine. 'At least rats and snakes and tarantulas don't pretend to be nice.'

'Your hand is really bad, Felix. We'd better get to school quickly.'

The school, like all those old fashioned schools you see in black and white movies, had a sanatorium.

'You're lucky that it was only as bad as it is,' said the kindly matron, who was washing my wound and then bandaging each finger up individually.

'Was I?' I said as I peered through the door of her office into the sick bay. Ten metal-framed beds were neatly arranged on the highly polished, wooden floor. Two boys were laid out flat. The first had his arms draped around the bedposts and his hands flat on the floor. The other had his legs folded over the end rail. They both looked like they'd had some kind of medieval torture performed on them with one of those things which pulls your arms in one direction and your legs in the other.

'Yes, those Janus-facers can have your hand off if you're not careful,' said the matron, as she finished dressing my wounds.

'Well, I certainly will be in future. Thank you, miss,' I said and then went off to Assembly, where we were all divided up into different classes.

A door at the back of the hall beside the stage was opened and we were led down the corridor, which seemed to go on forever.

'This way!' said Mrs Snapdragon, who had the one of those voices that told you that she didn't put up with any nonsense from anyone or anything, whether it be a dog, a child or a fellow guide. However, when she suddenly came to a standstill and looked back through her peering eyes at the three hundred pupils behind her, not a word needed to be spoken. Every single one of us knew instinctively what sort of behaviour she expected and we got ourselves into a perfectly straight line behind her. All chatter came to an abrupt halt.

'This door here, Springers, leads into Sage Class. Anyone who is a member of that class will peel off from the line and enter into it, as the rest of us continue walking down the corridor.'

Once the roll call of names, which included Edith, for that particular class had been read out, we did as was instructed. This little ritual continued until we finally reached Warrior Class, where my name was called out.

As I walked in through the door, I did take a quick peek into the class at the very end of the corridor – The House for Lost Souls, which was the one that Jermaine was put into. It looked just like one of those Victorian classrooms that I'd learnt about at primary school. There was even a cane and a dunce's hat on the teacher's desk. I couldn't imagine what on earth they got up to in there. I was thinking that someone should report them. Beating children and making them stand in the corner with a hat on their heads was definitely illegal and only happened in nightmares. But this was a **different** world and a **different** set of rules applied.

Our class was a bit like a Roman Arena and we were asked to sit in a circle around it.

'Good afternoon, Warriors,' said Mr O'Flaherty, as he welcomed us to his domain. I couldn't work out whether it was his bow tie, his multi-coloured waistcoat or the gaps in his teeth that stood out the most.

'This, I hope, will be a very auspicious day for all of you. No one,' he said, eyeing each member of our group with glee, 'will leave this room as the person that they came in here as.'

He left a pause here, just like TV presenters do when they wanted to create a bit of dramatic tension.

'I say this both literally – you'll see why in a minute – and metaphorically. Metaphorically because you will see such things in this room as you have never seen before. As I'm sure you all realise, you've been put into this house because of the nature of your past lives. You may not consider yourself to be a Warrior in your present incarnation but let me assure you, in no uncertain terms, that you were in your past lives.'

I imagined that this comment must have been directed at me. But then again, maybe everyone else was thinking that too.

'The circle that you are sitting around is – dare I say it – a magical circle,' continued Mr O'Flaherty. 'When you step inside it, it is possible not just to relive but also to **become** one of your former selves. Now you may all be looking at me and thinking – "That's Mr O'Flaherty. We saw him yesterday and he's exactly the same today." And how right you would be. However...'

Mr O'Flaherty stood very still and started to concentrate.

'If I allow myself to give in to my former self – which I won't do now – I could start to become...I think that you're getting the idea. As you know, the guides are not required to reveal anything about their previous lives. Indeed, it is better that we don't. So, if I could have a volunteer.'

My hand went up almost of its own accord.

'Felix, that would be excellent. Come into the centre of the circle.'

I did so and Mr O'Flaherty swapped places with me.

'Now, Felix. I think that you know a bit about one of your previous lives.'

'Yes. I found out about it yesterday.'

'Did you – and I need you to be honest now – know anything about this person, that you were, before yesterday?'

'A bit. Not much though.'

'Have you attempted to find out any more?'

'I would have done if I could have used a computer. But you can't do that here, can you?'

'Good. Now, Felix, I want you to close your eyes and answer some questions.'

'OK.'

'Do you have any memory of a life before this one?'

'Yes.'

'Tell us about it.'

'Well, I say "Yes", because I do now – or at least, as from yesterday – remember a bit about it. I was given some triggers by my guide and suddenly it all started to come back to me.'

'We're all ears, Felix.'

'Well, if I close my eyes, as I am doing at the moment, I can feel the biting wind blowing so hard against me that...I have to return to my tent and the warmth of my sleeping bag.'

Mr O'Flaherty threw a blanket over to me, which I proceeded to cover myself up in.

'It's only when the wind starts to drop a bit,' I continued, but in a voice nothing like my own, 'that I am able to come out from my shelter.'

As I pulled back the blanket, everyone who was sitting in the circle around me let out a gasp – with the exception of Mr O'Flaherty, who intervened:

'Edmund, can you tell us what you are planning for today?'

I had suddenly grown into this tall, strong man with an angular face and a New Zealand accent.

'Yes, of course. I am hoping that today will be the day that man has finally reached the top of the highest mountain in the world.

'Extraordinary,' said Mr O'Flaherty.

'It is. My fellow mountaineer, Tenzing Norgay, and I will set off to see if this really is humanly possible.'

'But you're risking your life in doing this, Edmund.'

'I know.'

'So why are you doing it, then?'

'Because it is there and because, quite simply, I have to.'

'Before you head off, would you mind sparing us a moment to tell us about your background,' said Mr O'Flaherty, who had started to sound like a newspaper reporter.

'Well, if you must know, before I came on this expedition, I kept bees.'

'And before that?'

'I was a navigator during the Second World War.'

'Why weren't you a pilot? A man of action like you.'

'Possibly because I didn't like the idea of fighting.'

'But I thought that you were a warrior.'

'A warrior does not have to fight people. He or she can take on major problems in the world. That's a much better reason to fight. To fight for what is good and to try to eliminate what is really bad.'

'Thank you, Edmund. And good luck with the final leg of your mission.'

A rope fell down in front of me and I grabbed it tightly with both hands. I climbed up it into an aperture above the ceiling and then disappeared. Once I was completely out of sight, Mr O'Flaherty called up to me.

'Thank you, Felix. We'll stop there.'

'But I'm not Felix.'

'You are now. Come back and join us please.'

I reappeared, looking like I did when I'd first entered the room. The only difference was that, instead of being shy and anxious, I now seemed strong, confident and victorious.

'That was terrific, Felix. If you'd like to…'

'Thank you,' I said graciously.

'We're going to see some others now. Come and join the circle.'

I then sat and watched with curiosity and amazement as a series of remarkable transitions happened in front of me and children turned into soldiers, rock musicians, nurses and film stars from another era. One of the best moments was when Rohan became Martin Luther King and gave his *I Have a Dream* speech. You probably know the one I mean. He dreams about white children and black children mixing happily together and everyone being equal. My other favourite bit was when Lily Thompson, who'd turned into George Harrison from The Beatles, started singing *Here Comes The Sun* and Sanjay Palmer went and joined her in the arena and became John Lennon.

The actual transformation didn't happen properly though until the lights went out momentarily. As they came back on again, John, with his round metal-framed glasses and corduroy cap, and George, in a collarless shirt and beads, were standing in front of the microphones, playing their guitars and singing *Give Peace a Chance*.

After working their way through a whole series of the old favourites, John made an announcement to the audience:

'For our next song, you can clap your hands, if you're poor that is. But if you're rich, you can rattle your jewellery.'

Everyone was cheering, shouting for more and joining in the choruses. At the end of *Hey, Jude* though, Mr O'Flaherty thought that it was time to draw things to a close.

'What a wonderful morning. I'm delighted to be able to confirm that everyone that has appeared in our arena today is a Sagacitor, which means that you all are Sagacitors too. And this has been your first real opportunity to get to understand what Sagacitors do. John Lennon and George Harrison weren't just pop stars. They also delivered the message of peace. Martin Luther King stood up for every black person in the world and fought for their rights. Rosa Parks did the same. Soldiers who committed extraordinary acts of bravery did so for their fellow countryman. No one knew that these people were Sagacitors, but their influence has affected the way that huge numbers of others have behaved. No one must ever know what we do on TWAWKI, but we must keep on doing it.'

There was a silence as we all took this in.

'And on that note,' said Mr O'Flaherty after a few seconds, 'you are free to go home, Warrior Class. I will see you all tomorrow.'

As I walked out of the room, I lingered in the corridor to see if I could hear anything from The Lost Soul's Room. It was completely quiet though and I couldn't even work out whether there was anyone still in there, until a high-pitched male voice cut through the silence.

'It's only on very rare occasions that we are forced to resort to the methods that we have just employed. They were not meant to cause you any harm, of course – merely to put you into another state of mind. One in which you might think differently about who you are and who you were. A bit of a shock often does the trick. If intimidation with the dunce's hat has not succeeded, we really do have to move on to the cane. I'm afraid to say that neither has worked in your case. This would suggest that whatever you did in your past life is too horrific for you to acknowledge. However, we do need to find out who you were. And we will! You may go home now, pack your belongings, such as they are, and be ready to start at the Other Campus tomorrow morning. You will be staying at the Other Accommodation as from tomorrow night – until further notice. Is that understood, Jermaine?'

I headed off down the hallway as quickly as I possibly could do without drawing attention to myself. It was essential that Jermaine did not know that I had overheard any of this.

As soon as I got home, I told Mrs Higgins that I'd had an exhausting day and that I was going straight to my room.

'Do you want a quick snack before you do? I'm just doing a fry up.'

'Oh, yes please, Mrs Higgins. That smells really good.'

'I do like to ensure that all my residents are happy. Do you want the full Oldsoulish?'

'Yes, please. Not too much bacon though.'

'Oh, no. We don't have bacon here. But we do have something like it. Trailcon. And these things, which bear a remarkable similarity to eggs, are called ovums. Oh, and of course we don't have mushrooms either. We have halooms. They're a different shape but they taste the same.'

Everything on my plate was so much better than it was anywhere on TWAWKI, on The World As We Knew It. This was the complete opposite to what my dad had cooked me. The trailcon melted in my mouth and tasted like salami. The ovums had a texture which was neither rubbery, runny or phlegmy but more like mushrooms –or halooms, as they were called here. It certainly took my mind off more troubling matters.

'This is really tasty, Mrs Higgins.'

'That's because of the environment. It's very pure here,' said Mrs Higgins proudly.

'Is that why the colours of all the trees and plants are all so bright here?'

'Yes, it always reminds me of those films that I used to watch back in TWAWKI, where everything was in technicolour.'

'Is that because it hasn't been polluted?'

'Yes. No global warming and all that sort of thing. Anyway, we won't sit around chatting. You want to get to bed. Would you like a bobolate?'

'Yes, please,' I said, realising how lucky I was to have someone so understanding. What she didn't get, though, was that this was not about me being tired but about me needing to avoid having a conversation with Jermaine. I sat on my bed and sipped on my mug of hot bobolate, which was a tasty blend of marshmallows and chocolate – although I wasn't really in the mood to appreciate it.

As I looked around the room, I suddenly spotted a book on the shelf, called *The History of Old Souls' Island*, which I pulled out and started to read. There was a section about some executions, that happened back in the Middle Ages, of people who had committed terrible crimes. There were rumours that these people's souls had not been able to move on and that their spirits still hung around the island to this day.

This gave me the creeps and as it was getting dark, I went to shut the curtains on the outside world. The sound of the sea beating against the cliff face was really calming though and I stood listening for a second. But another noise seemed to rise above it. Somebody crying? I opened my window to have a look and could see the silhouette of a boy standing by a cliff edge. It was Jermaine.

There was not a second to be wasted. I sneaked out of my room, down the stairs and out of the front door, picking up my shoes on the way. As soon as I had slipped them on, I ran through the grass over to Jermaine.

'Jermaine! What's wrong?'

'Nothing.'

'What do you mean – nothing?'

'Well, nothing that anyone can do anything about.'

I pretended not to know what he was talking about.

'That's a ridiculous thing to say.'

'No, it isn't. Not in my case. I can't change what I was in my past lives. They're over. It's not like I can go back to them, can I! If I was a murderer in my last life and the one before, what can I do about it now? You get me? I've done everything that I can to be good in this life and now I find that inside me is the heart of a murderer.'

'But how do you know that you were a murderer? You don't even know who you were.'

'What makes you say that?' retorted Jermaine, clearly taken aback.

'Because I heard…I overheard your conversations. You can't give in to this, Jermaine. I know that your guide is wrong.'

'Do you?'

'Yes. Yes, I absolutely do – in my heart. OK, you may have killed someone. Maybe you were in the army or something and you were just doing what was expected of you. Listen, have you ever in your life worried about a feeling inside you that you can't control?'

'What sort of feeling?' said Jermaine, quizzically.

'Anger, for instance. Have you ever felt something so strong inside you that you worry that it might lead you to do something terrible.'

'No.'

'I have.'

'Yeah, you can't control your anger sometimes. We all know that.'

'No, it's more than that. I sometimes worry that whatever it is that makes me feel the way I do is so strong that it will make me do something terrible. Not kill someone, but definitely hurt someone. Have you ever felt that?'

'No.'

'Well then, I am telling you that you are not a murderer. I know it. We have to get out of this place. Old Souls' Island is a good place. But every so often, some weird stuff starts happening – just like Mrs Higgins said. You and I aren't going to hang around to find out what it is though.'

'What are we going to do?' asked Jermaine.

'What are we going to do? What time is it back on Earth?'

'I don't know.'

'Two minutes past midnight. We've been away for two days, which is the same as two minutes back in TWAWKI time. We just need to find one of the collectors and ask them to take us back. Do you know where your one lives?'

'Yeah. That cottage there. On the other side of the bay,' said Jermaine, pointing towards the next headland.

'Well, we're going to go there right now.'

'Oh, my days. What about Edith though?'

'She'll be fine. She knows how to handle herself here. Anyway, she's been here before and she really wanted to come back. We'll tell your collector to give her a message.'

'OK. Shall we go and get our things?'

'You don't need anything from here, Jermaine. You're going home.'

7. Jo and Ivy

Fortunately, there was a light on downstairs in the cottage, where Jermaine's collector was living, and I peered through the window to check whether anyone was up. This was the type of place that I had only ever dreamed about, with its gnarled beams, carved oak furniture and crackling log-fire.

'There's a couple of girls with long black hair, sitting by the fire, but I can't see your collector. Do you think that I should knock on the window?'

Jermaine took a quick look.

'No, it's fine. That's Jo. Go ahead and knock, bruv.'

A boy with shoulder length hair swivelled his head round in surprise when I gave a polite couple of taps on the glass.

'It's Jermaine and Felix,' I called out as unthreateningly as possible.

The front door opened and Joseph welcomed us in.

'Hey, man. You gave me the shivers, man. We don't normally get visitors at this time of night.'

'Sorry, Jo,' I said, 'but we need your help – urgently.'

'OK. What do you want me to do? Take you back home or something,' he said jokingly.

'Well, yeah,' said Jermaine.

'Really?'

'Yes,' I repeated.

'Oh, I was only teasing, man. You can't be homesick already.'

'No, but Jermaine's got to go to the Other Campus tomorrow.'

'Oh, god. That's bad, man. Do you have to as well?'

'No, I'm all right. I've been identified as a Warrior,' I said, trying not to sound too smug about it.

'Cool!'

'For me – yes. But not for Jermaine. We've got to get him back home.'

'And you want me to take him?'

'Yes, please.'

'You don't understand, man. That would be like flying a private jet into Heathrow Airport without informing the flight controller. You've just picked the busiest time of year to do this. There's so much traffic coming in over the next few days.'

'Why's that?'

'Because there's all them second, third, fourth and fifth years coming in over the next week.'

'Really?'

'Yeah, of course. This place isn't just for you Springers. You've had a head start of course because you're new, but there's also all us lot who want to continue our education too. The only reason that I'm here early is because I'm a collector. Everyone else sets off from TWAWKI a few minutes later. It's

53

all very tightly scheduled. I might be able to sneak you back in a week's time when it all slows down again.'

'That'll be too late, though. Jermaine will be staying at the Other Accommodation by then,' I said, staring into the fire as if that might provide a solution.

'And no one gets out of there in a hurry. It's a complete nightmare,' said Jo.

'So what happens there?'

'Oh, you spend your life grafting for Subaltern. He's trying to get his Venetian palace restored and tarted up, using as many recruits like you as he can get hold of. Slave labour in other words. And he needs a lot of that at the moment while he's getting his swimming pool installed.'

'Did you say Venetian palace?'

'Yes, it and the canal that leads up to it were built several hundred years ago by some mad poet, who was really into Venice. It's dead cool to look at with all its weird pillars, arches and ornate carvings. And you get there by gondola.'

'Sounds great.'

'From the outside, yeah. And that's exactly how he's been allowed to keep it, because he pretends that its beauty has healing qualities which help troubled old souls work through their problems.'

'And do they?'

'No, man. They don't.'

'What about finding their past selves?' I said.

'Oh, no. He doesn't bother with any of that. If he did, he'd have to let them go back to the school. The guy just takes advantage of people like you, who don't know who they are and ensures that you continue not to know who you are.'

'That's bad, man. Why doesn't anyone stop him?' Jermaine chipped in.

'Because everyone – including the Head – is afraid of him.'

'So does this mean that Jermaine will have to spend the rest of the year slogging away for Mr Subaltern…and thinking that he's a murderer?'

'Not if we can help it, man.'

'What do you mean?'

'Well, we just need to join forces and do something about it.'

'Yes, we do,' said the girl with the really cool vibe about her, who had been sitting by the fire and listening intently to everything that had been said.

'Oh, this is Ivy, by the way. And this is her house.'

'Your house!' I exclaimed.

'Yeah, I know. Cool, eh! I'm in the second year and they've given me my own house.'

'That's extraordinary. No one would allow you to do that back in TWAWKI.'

'No, I know but they have…'

'…different rules here,' I cut in.

'Exactly. You've noticed,'

'Are you American?' I said, trying to work out her accent.

'Yeah. Kind of.'

'And are you a collector?'

'No.'

'So how come you're here now.'

'Oh, I didn't bother to go back last year.'

'Oh. Wow! So what would your mum and dad have thought when you were away for what…a whole year?'

'I don't know. They were probably quite relieved. I didn't really think about it, to be honest. I was asleep for all of that time. It's only six hours here on Old Souls' Island. Anyway, I just love being here. I've got my own house. I can do what I want. Who would want to go back and live with their crumby parents?'

As she said this, a Janus-facer suddenly appeared from behind the sofa and jumped onto her lap.

'Watch out!' I yelped.

'For what?' said Ivy, as a couple of cubs came and sat beside her.

'They're horrible. I got bitten by one of those.'

'Oh, did you?' she said, laughing and then smacking one of them on the backside, which made it whimper and cower in response.

'It's all right. Didn't hurt. Did it?'

'Not like Mr Subaltern then. He struck Jermaine with his cane.'

'Oh, no,' insisted Jermaine. 'He didn't, bruv. He stopped short just before he did.'

'You were lucky then,' said Ivy. 'He's nasty, man. Old Souls' Land is a cool place, but – like anywhere that's meant to be good – it attracts people who have malicious intentions. You don't have to be good to be an old soul. All it means is that you've been reborn a few times. These people see how they can manipulate the system and they do. Look, I know that you're going to stay there, so I don't want to frighten you too much. But Mr Subaltern is a lot worse than a man who just wants his swimming pool done. I should know. I've done my time in the Other Campus. I've seen him working his black magic and casting spells on everyone in the palace so that they behave like robots. He's **really** evil.'

'How come he's here then?' I said. 'You may not have to be good to be an old soul, but you do to be a Sagacitor.'

'Why do you think that the guides don't have to reveal who they were in a past life? He made that rule years ago, before most of his colleagues arrived here.'

'Why doesn't someone do something about him though?' I said, exasperated. 'Why is the head teacher afraid of him?'

'Oh, he's a really cool dude,' said Jo. 'But the only reason that he's been appointed to that position is because he has had lots of amazing previous lives – more so than anyone else here.

But he's only a year older than me. He's far too young to be able to control some of his manipulative staff.'

'So what do we do?'

'Tomorrow, Jermaine will go to the Other Campus as planned,' said Ivy. 'He's got no choice. We, meanwhile, will do everything in our power to get him out of there.'

'Is that all right, Jermaine?' I said tentatively.

'Yeah. Cool!' said Jermaine nervously as we went out of the door.

It was quite easy to find our way back as a pair of full moons meant that the island was well lit. Despite the fact that it was night time, all the vegetation still had a fluorescent quality. For a moment, we both felt inspired by our natural surroundings. The air was still and the sea was lapping gently against the rocks. If only our lives could be as simple and peaceful.

'It's so unfair that you have to go up to the Other Campus.'

'It'll be fine. Even though she says that Mr Subaltern is really evil, Ivy doesn't look like she's suffered too much. You get me? In fact, she seems to have everything she wants.'

'Yeah, I know. She's really cool.'

'Oh, do you fancy her – or something?'

'No, I don't mean that, you idiot! She's so much older than me for a start.'

'Yeah. About eighteen months.'

'Yeah, exactly. I just really envy her having her own house.'

'But you do like her as well,' said Jermaine, not wanting to let this one go.

'Yeah, yeah. I do.'

'Felix has got a girlfriend. Felix has got a girlfriend.'

'No, I have not got a girlfriend.'

'Yeah, you have, blud,' said Jermaine, wanting to get the final word in.

In fact, I couldn't really work out exactly what it was that I felt about Ivy. All I knew was that I really liked Jo and that I couldn't stop thinking about Ivy. I tried changing the subject.

'Do you think that this place has the same sort of…conditions as TWAWKI. It seems to have very similar qualities. I mean there's the moons up there. OK, one more than we have, but they're very similar…and there's a sun.'

'Only they don't call it the sun, they call it The Old Sol.'

'But we're the old souls,' I said, a bit confused.

'No, it's spelt differently: S-O-L. It's Latin for sun, apparently, and it's old because it's been around for twice as long as our sun.'

'But it's still very similar.'

'Yeah, a lot of things are. It's just the wildlife that's different. I think that most of the animals were brought from TWAWKI thousands of years ago.'

'What, like the ones on Noah's Ark?' I said, trying to imagine how they could possibly have transported them.

'Yeah, a bit like that. Then they acclimatised to this environment and evolved in their own peculiar way – like those weirdo creatures that have been following us. They're freaky, man. I mean most wild animals are either afraid of humans or they want to attack them.'

'Or they're just plain indifferent,' I added.

'Yeah, but these ones, bruv, have kept the same distance all the way. It's like they're spying on us or something.'

'No, I've never seen an animal behave like that,' I said as I observed what these long-necked, wolf-like creatures were doing. 'The people are quite similar though.'

'Course they are, man! The wildlife evolved here over thousands of years, whereas all the people started their lives in TWAWKI, didn't they?'

'Surely some people were born here.'

'No, bruv. That never happens.'

'Why not?'

'Because they might be new souls and you can't have **new** souls on **Old** Souls' Island, can you?'

'No, you can't!' I said sarcastically. 'That would be an outrage.'

Jermaine flipped into his silly posh accent.

'Personally, I'm going to find it very difficult going back to TWAWKI, old chap – having to talk to and mingle with all those new souls that inhabit that ghastly place.'

As we reached the house, a voice, from behind the front door, came out with an automatic response.

'That's exactly the reason why I decided to stay on here. Once you know what your station in life is, you don't want to have to reduce yourself to another level,' said Mrs Higgins in her most superior of voices, before changing her tone and getting down to brass tacks. 'And where have you two been, might I ask? It's way past your bedtimes, let alone the curfew.'

'Oh, sorry, Mrs Higgins. We just had to find out a few things because Jermaine's got to go to the Other Campus tomorrow.'

'Oh, that is a pity.'

'It's more than a pity. It's terrible. They don't treat people properly there. Do you know what they're really like, Mrs Higgins?'

'No, dear, I don't. I don't like to interfere.'

'Well, we better get to bed then. It's going to be quite some day tomorrow.'

'Yes, I expect it is,' said Mrs Higgins. 'I expect it is.'

8. The Venetian Palace

As I went out of the front door the next morning, Mrs Higgins seemed very dispirited.

'Well, we won't be seeing that young gentleman for a while,' she said.

'Has he gone?'

'Yes, someone came to collect him early this morning.'

'What, a collector?'

'No, no. Not in the sense you mean anyway. Just somebody from the palace – the ferryman.'

'Oh, well,' I said sadly and then headed off for school. Adrian was there to welcome me as usual.

'Good morning, Felix. All rested after yesterday's exploits, I hope.'

'After yesterday's exploits?' I retorted suspiciously. How did this boy know what I'd been up to? It's not like there was CCTV there. It could only be spies and I hadn't seen any of those. Not human ones anyway.

'Yes,' said my collector friend. 'Your conquest of Everest for a start.'

'Oh, yes. Of course.'

'You're a bit of a hero, Felix. Not many of us have had such an illustrious past as you.'

'Oh, really!'

'No. It'll be interesting to find out who you were before the mountain climber.'

'Well, I think that I kept bees and was a pacifist.'

'No, I mean in the life before you were Edmund Hillary.'

'Oh, I see. Yes, it will. Although I expect it'll take quite a while to get in touch with a more distant past.'

'Yes. About five minutes to be exact.'

'What do you mean?'

'Oh. They haven't told you then?'

'No, they haven't.'

'Well all I can say is that today is going to be a big day for you. The Day of Revelation.'

I found myself a space in the crowded hall and waited, as usual, for the head teacher to appear. Although I was surrounded by people, I was as lonely and self-conscious as I had thought I would be. There was no one around me that I knew. What with Jermaine at the Other Campus, Edith nowhere to be seen and my new friends still at home, there was no one to talk to.

'Hey, guys. Look who it is. The man who thinks that he's a hero,' called out a voice from behind me.

'Oh yes. It's the one who did none of the hard work but took all the glory.' said another.

'What do you mean?' I said.

The two boys then came and stood either side of me, looking like a comedy duo. Sanjay was small and slight, like me. George was the opposite. Sanjay was the one who'd turned out to have been one of The Beatles in his previous life. He had seemed really nice when I first met him. But, of course, people hardly ever show their true colours on the first few days of school.

'There were fourteen other people on that expedition and they all got as close as they could to the top. It was just that one of them, and his Sherpa who he couldn't have done it without, pushed his way past everyone else and...' said Sanjay.

'What you talking about? That's not how it was,' I exclaimed.

'You mean that that's not the way that you choose to remember it,' said George.

'No.'

'Because when you go into your former self, you can only see it from your point of view. That's why,' said Sanjay.

'Maybe.'

'Can't wait to find out who you were before that. Probably some big fraudster or something,' said George.

I didn't have a chance to answer as the head teacher was making his entrance down the staircase and the whole assembly had gone quiet.

After his customary chit chat, he told us all about the Day of Revelation, his favourite moment of the week – if not the term. Many of us would be wondering how we could possibly find out who all our previous incarnations were – just in one day? The answer was, of course that once you knew what your last life was, you could find out from all the records what the other ones were before that. If you were an old soul in your last life, you would have probably come to this island then as well.

It suddenly felt like all those three-dimensional carvings on the walls were peering down at me. I wondered where each of them was now. Had they continued to be reborn? Were any of their souls inhabiting the kids in this hall? Had anyone here been

William Shakespeare or Florence Nightingale in a previous life? That would probably all soon be revealed – to the individuals in question anyway.

Our names were then called out, as they had been on the first day, and I was summoned almost immediately to see my personal guide.

'This is all a bit worrying,' said Asha, as I closed the door of Room 21 behind me.

'What is, miss?'

'Your records. They're worrying, but they're also somewhat confusing.'

'Are they?'

'Yes, they don't really make any sense.'

'Oh.'

'Mrs Snapdragon read them out to me this morning. I'm not going to tell you what they said. That will only make things worse than they already are. And I want to look into this. So I suggest that you go back home now and don't come back until tomorrow. That will give me time to investigate this. Have you anything in particular that you want to do?'

This had to be the perfect opportunity to see if I could find out where the Other Campus was, while everyone else was still in school.

'Explore the island...maybe?'

'Good idea. We shall see you tomorrow then.'

I headed back down the path and past Mrs Higgins' house. When I got to the place where I had first arrived on Old Souls' Island, I paused for a moment, sat down and tried to remember what I had felt like then. So much had happened in the last three days, which back home in TWAWKI was only three minutes. Only three minutes had passed on TWAWKI since I'd left! The time it takes to make a cup of tea.

I then glanced back behind me to see five or six of the long-necked, wolf-like creatures – the ones that Jermaine and I had seen the night before. It was like playing grandmother's footsteps. They suddenly stopped still and nonchalantly pretended that they were minding their own business, looking in another direction.

As I set off again, I could see for the first time what a mish-mash of history there was on this island. I passed an 18th century wool mill, which was nestled in between a Tudor cottage on one side and a Victorian house on the other. Old souls had, of course, been coming here for years. Beyond all of that, I climbed through the remnants of a Roman village and past their recreation of Stonehenge, which looked like it was the colour it should be. It certainly wasn't red anyway. And then eventually, I spotted the canal.

The palace was even better than I had thought it would be, with its rows of arches on every level and ornate carvings – all reflected in the water directly in front of it. I didn't think that I had ever seen anything quite so beautiful. However, my excitement died within seconds. Perhaps Mr Subaltern's whole reason for having this palace was, as Ivy had said, to seduce you into thinking that it was a good place.

At the end of the canal was a boat with a big, beefy, old man lounging inside it. Although he was wearing a hood over his head, I could still see his long grey beard and his bulbous eyes staring out at me.

'Excuse me,' I said cautiously.

'Yes,' replied the man.

'Is it possible for me to get to the palace?'

'Not unless you've been requested, no.'

'I just wanted to visit my friend.'

'What's his name?'

'Jermaine…Jermaine Toussaint.'

There was no response except for the fact that the ferryman pushed the boat, with his long, wooden punt, out into the water and headed off in the direction of the palace. I looked back out to sea and watched a flock of thirteen yellow birds, gliding alongside the coastal path in a 1–2–4–6 formation, shaped like a triangle. I'd never seen that on TWAWKI. As the leader flew towards a tree and perched herself on a branch, the others followed suit, six landing on one side of her and six on the other. Why couldn't humans be as in tune with each other as that?

I turned back to see the old man returning with what looked like an empty boat. However, as he tied it up to one of the poles, Jermaine suddenly appeared from underneath an oil skin.

'Alright, bruv,' he said as he stepped onto the bank.

'Can we…?'

'What?'

'Go for a walk or something.'

'Oh, yeah. Sure,' said Jermaine with a giggle, as we wandered out of earshot of the ferryman. 'He's alright.'

'Really!...What time's he knock off?'

'Six o'clock.'

'Great! I reckon that if I come back in a couple of days' time – at night – that you could swim down the canal to here, where I'll be waiting for you. Then we could get you back to Jo's and he could take you home.'

'But why would I want to do something like that?'

'To get out of here, of course.'

'Oh, I see.'

'You can't stay here,' I whispered. 'You heard what Ivy said about Mr Subaltern. He's evil.'

'No, I…'

'Well, he may not appear to be at the moment. But he…'

'No, he's cool, man.'

'But he beat you with a cane.'

'No. That was just pretending, bruv.'

'No, it wasn't. How can you call holding a cane…?'

'You weren't there, man. How do you know? He's cool. OK.'

65

'Jermaine. You can't stay here. You have no idea what could happen to you if you stay. You're just being seduced into…into a false sense of…'

'Security? No, I'm not. It's going to be good for me…Anyway, got to go back in now.'

'Is this all the time they'll let you out for?'

'No, of course not. I can come and go as I please,' said Jermaine assertively.

'So why have you got to go in so quickly?'

'To finish my game of chess.'

'I'm coming back again,' I said forcefully.

'Do as you please. I'm not leaving though, not until I'm ready, blud. Understand!' he said and started walking back to the gondola.

'But that's going to be too late. Don't you understand? You idiot!' I said, grabbing Jermaine's collar to stop him from going.

'What did you call me?'

'Sorry. I was just getting…'

'Angry. I know,' said Jermaine, who understood better than anyone how to stop me in my tracks.

'Ok. I'll see you in a few days' time then.'

'OK.'

'Who's winning by the way?' I called, as Jermaine got into the boat.

'Who do you think?' Jermaine said with a smile on his face as he disappeared back down the canal towards his grand, majestic residence.

So, my best friend was not just in the hands of an evil manipulator but also under his spell. There was no doubt that he was being brainwashed. The way he responded when I mentioned the cane was a complete give-away. There was absolutely no doubt that Mr Subaltern had beaten or at least threatened Jermaine with a cane. I'd heard it all – with my own ears!

The canal and the Venetian palace had for a moment had the same effect on me too though. I'd fallen for its charms. That must be what it was there for. That is why Mr Subaltern had taken it over. It was so easy to be seduced by its power.

I looked to see if there were any of those long-necked wolves following me. No sign of them for the moment, but there was a girl, slightly darker-skinned than Jermaine and definitely younger than him or me, who was doing a worse job of attempting to look innocent than the wolves had.

One moment, she'd pretend to be playing a game of jumping back and forward across a stream and then, as soon as I turned my back, I could tell that she'd be stopping and staring at me. Every time I looked round again, she'd try and return to her stupid game, but she'd miss her footing and end up in the stream.

Everywhere I went, I was being stalked. But by who? Who were the animals and this girl working for? Presumably Mr Subaltern. What would happen if I tried to shake this kid off? I couldn't believe that I was in this situation, which belonged in a world of espionage. It's not something that children did – spy on each other! It was even weirder to think that animals were doing it as well.

9. Temper Tantrums

'Well, I think that you should be going back to school this morning,' said Mrs Higgins, as I came down the stairs. 'No one's said anything different.'

'OK, I will then, Mrs Higgins…um…Mrs Higgins.'

'Yes, dear.'

'Is Old Souls' Island the only land mass in Old Souls' World?'

'Oh, no, dear. Old Souls' World has got lots of islands on it with lots of different cultures and languages. You've probably noticed that only English is spoken here though. Mind you, that's not to say that it's always spoken as it should be spoken.'

'How's that?'

'Correctly!' she said, enunciating every syllable. 'Anyway, you better get off now or you'll be late.'

'See you this evening, Mrs Higgins,' I said and headed off towards the tree tunnel. When I got to school, there was a group of Springers outside who were playing some kind of game, which involved being dressed up in suits of armour. Two people would stand several feet apart and throw things like fruit, sticks, dead birds and old hairbrushes at each other. Every so often, there would be a cheer to show that someone had won, at which point someone else would take their place. But I couldn't figure out how this all worked and what it was you had to do to win. So I headed into the hall. Out of the corner of my eye, I could see the two boys who had taunted me the other day.

'They let you back in again,' one of them whispered in my ear.

'How the mighty have fallen,' said the other.

'Yeah, all the way from the top of Everest,' said the first.

'And down into the rubbish tip!'

I decided to ignore all of this as there was so much more to untangle elsewhere that was even worse than this. The head teacher arrived at the bottom of the stairs and told those of us who had come early that there would be no formal assembly today and that we would be with our personal guides first off.

'Come in, Felix,' called out Asha, as I knocked on the door of Room 21.

'Thank you.'

'How are you today?'

'All right, considering...'

'Yes, your records. We're still looking into them...someone may have tampered with them. We don't know.'

'Asha,' I said, feeling that I could be a bit more relaxed with her. 'You said on the first day that I have to be truthful.'

'Yes.'

'Well, can I say this to you in...um...'

'In confidence. Yes. Say what you have to say. I won't tell a soul. Not an old one anyway. And that's all there are here.'

'Thank you. Well, I'm worried that some of the Sagacitors here may not be as good as they're supposed to be. In fact, that's a...a...'

'An understatement?'

'Yes. There's a lot of evil here on this island and I want to go back home. But I can't until I've rescued Jermaine.'

'He's at the Other Campus. Is that right?'

'Yes and he's being brainwashed.'

'And how might that be happening?' said Asha, clearly unconvinced.

'Mr Subaltern has been playing with their minds.'

'Felix, that is quite an accusation that you've just made there.'

'Maybe. But I think that it's true.'

'On what grounds?'

'I saw Jermaine yesterday and he says that he's really enjoying living at the Venetian palace.'

'Well maybe he is. That's hardly a reason to suspect that his mind is being played with.'

'No.'

'You need to be very careful who you say this to. Going around making accusations like that could get you into a lot of trouble.'

'I suppose so.'

'Now, today we were supposed to be looking at you in this life. We've looked at you in your last life and unfortunately we don't have the notes to find out who you were before that. So we are going to concentrate on you, as you are right now.'

'OK.'

'Clearly, you have a very suspicious nature, but is there anything that you struggle with in particular about yourself?'

'Anger. I can get angry and I can lose control.'

'Have you ever ended up getting into a fight as a result of this?'

'Yes...a couple of times, when I've got...'

70

We were interrupted by a knock on the door though.

'Could you get that?'

I opened the door to find George and Sanjay, the boys who had been teasing me earlier, standing there like a picture of innocence.

'Excuse me, miss. I'm so sorry to interrupt you but the head teacher has asked to see Felix Featherstone,' said George.

'Oh yes, of course. You better go with them then, Felix. I'll see you later,' said Asha.

I shut the door behind me and followed the boys along the gallery until they got to the staircase.

'Oh, he gets angry, does he? The Pacifist!' whispered Sanjay into my ear.

'We better be careful that we don't rub him up the wrong way then,' said George.

'No, we don't want him getting into a temper tantrum with one of us.'

'Have you been listening?' I asked.

The boys sniggered.

'Hang on. Have I really got to go and see the head teacher?'

The boys sniggered again.

'What are you playing it? What's your problem, for god's sake?'

Despite all my efforts to avoid this, I had flipped from a state of mind that I had some control over to one that I definitely did not.

'How dare you treat me like this. You don't even know me. What have I done to you to make you want to do this to me?'

'Existed, mate. Existed,' said George.

I could feel myself beginning to well up.

'Oh, perhaps you should go back to Mummy. She'll kiss you better,' said George.

This prompted the other one to pretend to be 'Mummy', putting his arms around me. I decided not to give them the pleasure of letting them know that I didn't have a 'mummy' though.

'But Mummy's not here. Do you want me to kiss you? There, there, my poor little diddums.'

There was no stopping me now. I grabbed hold of George's arms and thrust him away. The push was enough to send him a few yards down the corridor and George, wanting to make it look a bit more dramatic, 'accidently-on-purpose' collapsed onto the floor. His pre-planned falling-over act had not taken into account that this would take place at the top of the stairs however. The result was, of course, that he went tumbling, hitting his head as he got to the bottom.

I didn't call out: 'How the lowly have fallen!', but I said it to myself. In the meantime, everyone had come out of their rooms to find out what all the noise was about. Mrs Snapdragon arrived at the scene just in time to see me standing at the top of the stairs, looking victorious, whilst my supposed victim was writhing in in agony below me.

'Felix Featherstone,' she called out. 'Lost Souls' Room. **Now**!'

'Sit down,' she snapped as she led me into this disturbing room.

'Whereabouts, miss?' I said as I eyed all the Victorian benches.

'Wherever you like,' she answered sharply.

'Thank you, miss,' I said, sitting down directly opposite her desk.

Not a word was uttered for the next five minutes. I looked up into space whilst Mrs Snapdragon read through my notes. It felt a bit like going to the doctor.

'So, Felix,' she said eventually. 'You should by all accounts remember this place.'

'Yes, I took a quick peek when we passed it yesterday.'

'I don't mean then. I mean in your previous incarnations. According to your notes, you have been a frequent visitor and in fact were one of the first occupants just after it was built.'

'When was that?'

'In Victorian times, of course.'

'Oh, yes. Of course.'

'This is all very worrying. I had given you the benefit of the doubt. I had thought there was something wrong with your records. But not after what has just happened.'

'No, miss.'

'According to your records, all your previous lives – with the exception of your last one – have been extremely disturbing. Strange that you should have had such an exemplary existence last time round. That's almost unheard of. Old souls change by degrees. A complete turnaround is almost impossible. There must have been darker things going on with Sir Edmund Hilary than the world ever got to hear about.'

She stopped and looked at me as if I should have been able to provide an answer to this.

'Well, were there?'

'I don't know, miss…and I don't know anything about the lives that I had before that.'

'You will in good time. We'll take you through them.'

'Yes, miss,' I said.

'Felix,' she said, looking me straight in the eye. 'Old Souls' Island is generally a very happy place. It has been used over the years to enable people to find the true depths of who they really are. We nurture souls here and bring out the best in people, in order that they can return to TWAWKI and perform their duties as Sagacitors. But just occasionally we come across someone like you who keeps being reborn, not because they are good but because they are bad. Bad old souls. No one knows why this happens, but it may be because there is hope that they can finally be good. You have perhaps proved that in your last life. Now you have to prove it in this one. Otherwise, there will be no possibility of you being a fully fledged Sagacitor. Anyway, you'll go back home now to Mrs Higgins, get your stuff and then you'll be taken to the Venetian palace.'

'But that's evil.'

'What makes you say that?'

'People have told me that. Its beauty on the outside covers up the corruption on the inside.'

'Well, I don't know who you've been talking to, but they're just trying to scare you. Now get back to Mrs Higgins' and I'll send someone to collect you within the hour.'

10. Brain Washing

Mrs Higgins wasn't in when I returned, but the creepy looking ferryman, dressed in black today, was waiting outside the front door.

'Are you here to take me to the palace?'

'That's right,' said the man, without even looking at me.

'I'll be with you in five minutes then.'

'Make sure it's no more than that.'

'It won't be, sir.'

There was an old leather suitcase in my room – just the right size for the few belongings and clothes that I had accumulated since I had been on Old Souls' Island. Having thrown everything in that I thought that I would need, I ran down the stairs and out of the front door.

'Alright. Let's go,' said the man, who then proceeded to walk at speed along the cliff path without uttering another word. There was clearly no room for conversation, so I just looked out to sea and watched the fishermen pulling up their nets to reveal assortments of fish, spanning all the colours of the rainbow. Further out towards the horizon, there were passenger boats disappearing into the distance. Where were they going? Were all the other islands in Old Souls' World as peculiar as this one could be?

As we got to the Roman Village, Stonehenge suddenly came into view – in all its terrible glory. Although it wasn't blood red, it was looking decidedly pinkish. This was bad. It made me realise that it wasn't just schoolboy arguments that were going on. There was something really disturbing happening and the barometer had definitely registered it. I wanted to ask the ferryman, but he still had that face which said he wasn't prepared to talk to anyone.

'Right. Jump in,' said the man, finally breaking the silence, as he held on to the end of the gondola. The grey-bearded man then punted the boat down the canal, as if we were part of a funeral procession. I felt like I was being transported from one part of this world, which I had now become accustomed to, to an altogether much darker and stranger environment. Despite the fact that the palace was looking as beautiful on the outside as it had done the day before, it was not in any way inviting. I sat and listened as the boat creaked and the ferryman's punt dipped slowly and ominously into the water.

Once the gondola had been secured to a post, I climbed out onto the palace forecourt and through one of its arches. As soon as my feet had touched the ground, my ferryman untied the rope and was off back down the canal again.

The front door opened a fraction and all I could make out was a pair of eyes staring out at me.

'Hello.'

'Oh, hello,' I replied.

'Can we help you?'

'Yes, I've been sent here by Mrs Snapdragon.'

'Name?'

'Felix Featherstone.'

'Come in. Someone will show you to your room in a minute.'

'I'll do that,' said a voice, which I immediately recognised.

'Jermaine!'

'Yes. I heard you were coming. Follow me!'

Jermaine grabbed my suitcase and headed up a stone spiral staircase, which seemed to go on forever. As we climbed up to the top, I was trying to work out how affected by this place my friend had become.

'I hope everything is to your satisfaction, sir. Any problems, just ring for room service.'

'Room service?'

'Indeed, sir. As soon as you are ready, Mr Subaltern will see you in his office. When you have finished with him, perhaps you would care to join us in the Billiards Room for a glass of sherry, followed by a little bit of a knockabout.'

'A glass of sherry? Are you kidding me?'

'That is merely the term that the residents use for it. It does, however, taste like sherry – rich, thick and fruity but without the alcohol.'

'Jermaine, what is this?'

'This is the Venetian palace, sir. We look forward to your company in the Billiards Room. In the meantime, we hope that you enjoy your stay,' said Jermaine as he pulled the door shut behind him.

I started to unpack a bit, but I was more confused than ever. Was this my friend play-acting as he often did or was this my friend believing that he was living in some kind of grand hotel? It was hard to tell, but I didn't have much time to think about it as I was interrupted by a knock on the door.

'Felix!' called out a voice.

'Yes.'

'Mr Subaltern wants to see you in his office in five minutes.'

'OK. Where is it?'

'Next floor down.'

So I had been summoned by the man himself. This was my big moment. The meeting with the monster.

The door of the office was open, so I walked straight in. Mr Subaltern was sitting at a large antique desk with a view of the canal behind him. The room was dimly lit. So I could only really make out that the man was small and skinny – and had a sweaty forehead.

'Ah, Felix,' he said in his high-pitched voice as he jumped up to shake hands with me. 'Welcome to the club.'

'The club?' I thought. That sounded a bit sinister. 'Thank you,' was all I could think of saying in response.

'I'm delighted you're here. You're a very curious case and I do love a challenge.'

'A challenge? Me?'

'Yes. We've never had anyone like you before. It's going to be fascinating to get working on you.'

What did he mean – get working on me? This was getting even more sinister. Brainwashing? Brain-manipulating? Brain-bending?

'Get working on me?'

'Yes, to find out about your previous lives.'

'When will you start doing that?' I said, as my shoulders started to twitch.

'As soon as you're ready. We'll give you a couple of days to settle in, get to know the gang and the routine here and then...Oh, I gather that you've already got a friend here.'

'Yes. Jermaine Toussaint.'

'Yes. He's responding very well to the therapy.'

'Is he?' I said anxiously. I didn't like the sound of that at all, particularly after what Ivy and Jo had said and the way Jermaine had just been behaving. 'Do I have to have this therapy?'

'No, of course not. You're here on Old Souls' Island of your own free will. We can't make you do anything. If you want to go back to TWAWKI, well then – so be it! However, I would strongly advise that you went through with our treatment programme. It has fantastic results, not just for here but also for when you return back home. You'll be bringing back the elixir all right.'

'Bringing back the elixir?'

'Yes. It's a phrase used in mythology. In your case, it means that you'll be taking back something very rich and empowering when you return to TWAWKI. However, if you were to return now…'

'Oh, I see.'

'Well, it's been very good to meet you properly, Felix. I've heard so much about you,' said Mr Subaltern, as he shook hands with me. 'I suggest that you go and join the other reprobates now for a bit of…I don't know…whatever high jinks they're currently up to.'

'Thank you, sir,' I said nervously and then left the room.

'Oh, leave the door open. I like to keep an eye on what's going on,' said Mr Subaltern with a bit of a chortle.

'Yes, sir.'

No one had told me where anything was. So I decided to explore my new environment and headed downstairs to the ground floor. Doors to rooms were open, so I could see what my fellow 'reprobates' were up to. Some were reading, some playing chess or Monopoly whilst others were drinking sherry, as they called it, and having a game of billiards. I liked the calm atmosphere. I always liked silence. But this was a different type of silence. It was…the only word I could think of and the one I kept using…*sinister*.

What had Mr Subaltern done to all of these children to make

them behave like this. If they were anything like me in a free situation like this, they'd be screaming and running down corridors. But these guys seemed like they'd been zombified.

I had to get out of here. Now! Before it was too late. Before anything was done to me. Fortunately, Jermaine hadn't noticed me, as he was too concentrated on making his break on the billiard table. So I headed off back up the stairs and past Mr Subaltern's office.

'Can I help you, Felix?'

'Oh, no. I'm alright.'

'You look lost.'

'No, I thought I might go back to my room. I haven't unpacked properly yet.'

'Have you brought a trunk or something?' said Mr Subaltern with icy sarcasm.

'No, just a small suitcase.'

'Well. I'm sure that that can wait. If you don't want to mix with your fellow inmates, perhaps we should get started on your therapy.'

'Alright,' I said nervously.

'So – to begin with – we all know what your last life was. At least, every member of Warrior Class does.'

'Yes, they do.'

'But what about the one before that?'

'I've no idea, sir.'

'No, of course you've no idea. It's almost impossible to automatically return to the 'life before last' without some prompting. But it is absolutely essential that we find out who it was. Until we do, we can't train you up to be a fully fledged Sagacitor. A Sagacitor whose intentions are evil is capable of doing an awful lot of damage in the world...Now I'm going to give you some...'

I was shaking visibly now, terrified that Mr Subaltern might try and hypnotise me. How could I possibly stop him? I could ask to be sent back to TWAWKI, but Old Souls' Land was in terrible danger and I had to do something about it. There was no way that I was going home until I'd rescued Jermaine from this evil place either. So I had to remain on the island, but not here in this creepy palace – that was for sure. A temper tantrum, of course! That's how I usually got myself out of a situation? Not the type that I had supposedly had with George and Sanjay, but just enough of one to be a nuisance and to disturb the calm of this environment. It would not be difficult for me to have an outburst and create a scene. I was angry enough as it was – just being in this situation.

'Actually, I think that I would like to go and join the 'reprobates' after all.'

'Oh, good. I'm not going to stop you.'

I went back down the stairs and made a bee line straight for the Billiards Room, where Jermaine had just potted his final ball.

'Good timing, Felix. Grab yourself a sherry and we'll have a game of something.'

'Thanks, old boy,' I said in my posh voice, playing along with my friend, but still worried about his state of mind.

'Could we play Monopoly?'

'If that's what you want.'

As we sat down at the table, I noticed how obedient and well behaved they all were. Not one of them was leaning back on their chairs in a chilled manner or rabbiting away to their mates. Kids could be quiet at times, but not like this. There was something almost **too** well-behaved about them, as they started to count out the shares of money and deal out the relevant cards. I was more concentrated than I had ever been. It was going to be a difficult game to play. On one level, I needed to look as though I was wanting to be competitive and on another, I had to make a move which would suddenly lose me all my money. Half an hour into the game, I was four places away from Park Lane, where Jermaine had put two of his hotels. Here was my chance. I just needed to fix the dice when no one was looking.

'Actually, I think I might have another one of those sherries.'

'OK, I'll get you one,' said Jermaine.

I then dropped a couple of my cards under the table.

'Don't worry. I'll pick that up,' said Georgia.

'Oh, thanks,' I said, making sure that my foot was firmly on top of them.

'Felix, your foot's on the cards,' called up Georgia from underneath the table.

'Sorry,' I said with a gesture that sent a glass of sherry flying and wetting Dryden's shirt and trousers. Now was my opportunity to make a fake throw.

'Two and two. Four!' I said, placing the dice on the table and taking my foot off the cards.

'But you didn't throw them,' said Dryden who was trying to get the sherry stain out of his shirt.

'Didn't I?'

'No, you just put them down.'

'Oh, sorry. I'll do it again,' I said, putting my foot back down on the cards.

'Oh, why don't you go and get a cloth from Mr Subaltern while I have my go.'

'Oh, yeah. Good idea,' said Dryden.

'Oh, no,' I cried out as Dryden left the room. 'I've got four again. One, two, three, four…Park Lane.'

'Brilliant. That's one thousand five hundred pounds, please,' said Jermaine, returning with the sherry.

'But I haven't got that much.'

'Well, you'll just have to sell some of your properties.'

'That's going to leave me with nothing. That's completely ridiculous. I hate this stupid game,' I screamed, throwing the board into the air with everything that was on it, just at the moment that Dryden returned, accompanied by Mr Subaltern.

'Felix Featherstone. My office!'

'Yes, sir.'

Mr Subaltern swivelled round and returned back down the corridor. I followed immediately behind, looking particularly sheepish. Little did Mr Subaltern realise how thrilled I was that everything had gone to plan.

'Could you explain exactly what you hoped to achieve with this outburst?' said Mr Subaltern as he shut the office door behind him.

'I got frustrated, sir. I got angry.'

'And were you happy with this?'

'No, sir.'

'I would have thought that having been sent here for that very reason, the least you might have done would be to rein it in a bit.'

'I know, sir,' I said, not wanting to reveal what my true intentions had been.

'It worries me to think that I might have had to have sent you over the bridge.'

'What's that, sir?'

'Over here, Felix,' said Mr Subaltern, taking me out of the office and pointing at a corridor, with windows either side, which appeared to go over the canal. 'We call it the Bridge of Sighs.'

'Why's that, sir?'

'Because it leads to the old cells and dungeons. Like the one in Venice, it was originally built as a passage between a palace and a prison. The convicted men and women sighed as they crossed it. In days gone by, they didn't just lock people up down there, they executed them as well.'

'You don't do that now, do you?'

'Of course not, Felix. But we do have occasion to put people down there for a few hours to cool off.'

This place was getting worse by the minute. I couldn't work out which I disliked the most – the therapy or the cells.

'However, I've just had a call from the school. Apparently George and Sanjay have admitted to being highly provocative towards you. They have accepted full responsibility for what happened today.'

'Thank you, sir.'

'In the light of that, the school will accept you back.'

'Thank you, sir.'

'You would get much more concentrated therapy here than you would there when it comes to approaching your past lives. But since, within one hour of your residence here, you have managed to completely disrupt the calm that I have worked so hard to achieve, I have no other option than to ask you to leave the Venetian palace.'

'Yes, sir,' I said, attempting to disguise my overwhelming relief.

'The ferryman awaits.'

'Thank you, sir.'

'Off you go and get your suitcase. Lucky you didn't unpack it.'

11. Battle Plans

Once I'd been dropped off at the end of the canal, I wasted no time in making my way over to Ivy and Jo's to tell them about the palace. As I got close to the cottage, I suddenly heard this clacking sound, coming from behind me and I nearly jumped out of my skin as a skateboard narrowly missed hitting me. Its rider then niftily scooted around me and promptly came to a standstill.

'Hi, Felix,' said Ivy, taking off her helmet.

'Oh, I was just coming to see you. Did you…?'

'Yes, we've heard. Past records. Hissy fits. The palace! You see what I mean about that place. It's really bad.'

'Yes, everyone's in a trance there. No one, apart from me, seemed to be worried about what was happening to them.'

'Yes, if you disrupt the calm, he doesn't want you in there.

That's how you get out. But you have to do that before he casts his spell on you,' said Ivy.

'Or puts you in the cells,' I added.

'Yes, people get locked up for weeks.'

'Well, hours anyway. The only good thing was that the kids I saw weren't being treated like slaves.'

'You believed that charade, did you? Don't worry, they'll all be back to work again tomorrow.'

'We have to do something about the place.'

Ivy did not respond but just stared into my eyes.

'Do you fancy a bobolate?' she said after a few moments.

'Oh, yes please.'

'Come in then.'

Ivy went through to the kitchen and I went to join Jo, who was snuggled up next to the log fire, which was crackling away as always.

'Hi, man. Take a pew. How ya doin'?'

'OK. Although, not really.'

'What's the problem, man?'

I told him all about how I thought Jermaine was being seriously brainwashed and asked him if he could get him back to TWAWKI. But, apparently, it wasn't as easy as all that.There were certain procedures that you had to go through first, like getting your haircut, for instance. You had to be returned in the same condition that you were collected in. That's why they took photographs of you on the first day. You might have grown a bit. There's nothing anyone could do about that, but the haircut's always the big give away. Not that mine had changed much since I'd left home.

'So how come you didn't have to chop that lot off?' I said, pointing at his long floppy hair.

'Because I grew all this in TWAWKI before I came back. It was really cool too because my parents thought that I was rebelling in the same way as hippies used to. So I could really feel my previous existence coming through, man.'

'That's really cool.'

'Yeah, it was. Anyway, I'll have a think about Jermaine. We could give it a go.'

'We could,' said Ivy coming in with the bobolates. 'But what good is that going to be for the rest of us on the island?'

'It'll be good for him.'

'Felix, I didn't want to have to tell you this before. But, it seems that the time has come. Why do you think that Subaltern's getting away with manipulating those kids in the way that he is?'

'Simple! All the other staff are afraid of him.'

'Do you really think that that is enough to stop a whole body of people, whose job it is to keep the world in balance, from fighting for what they believe to be right.'

'Yeah, man,' interjected Jo. 'They say that their mission is to ensure good wins over evil!'

'Exactly,' said Ivy. 'Anyone who is devoting their life to doing that is not going to be defeated by…Do you know what subaltern means, by the way?'

'No.'

'It means second-in-command. And that's all he is. He's a little man who thinks he's big. No one's really going to be afraid of him. There are far more powerful forces at play here than him. Do you really think that your past lives were so bad that they weren't able to tell you about them this morning?'

'No, I don't.'

'Someone's obviously tampered with your records.'

'Yeah, that's what I thought and that's what my guide felt as well.'

'Well, she was right. There is a large and terrifying network of evil here on this island and we can either walk away from it or take it on ourselves.'

'Is that why you're still here?'

'Too right it is. Don't forget. It's not just here that's going to suffer, but the whole of TWAWKI. This network of evil is trying to infiltrate the minds of Springers and corrupt them. Jo feels the same.'

'Yeah, man. They tampered with my records too. Only I knew who else I'd been and the head teacher – before he became the Head – verified what I said. So I was able to keep going to the school. But there's some weird stuff going on there. Not from him, not from Mrs Snapdragon, not from Mr O'Flaherty, but some of the others…Oh, boy!'

'So what should I do?' I asked.

'Go back tomorrow. See what they have to say. You don't have to join our little coven, so to speak, but god help you if you don't.'

'This is all getting too much for me. I don't think that I can handle this anymore. What's going on here? Is Mrs Higgins OK?'

'Yeah, yeah. You'll be fine with her. She's just in her own space, man. Why don't you go back there now and rest, man. It's been a long day.'

'It sure has.'

'Your wolveraffes are waiting!' announced Ivy.

I stood there a bit bemused for a second and then caught on to what she meant.

'Oh. Is that what they are?'

'Yes, of course.'

'Do you mean to say they were…guarding me?'

'What else would they be doing? Spying on you?' said Ivy.

'Well, I suppose that wouldn't be much use – unless they could talk.'

'Exactly. They do my bidding and they do it very efficiently.'

'Well, thank you…At least there's something that I can trust on this god-forsaken, mind-boggling island.'

12. Sixes and Sevens

Mrs Higgins had done herself proud at the dinner table that night and her Old Souls' Pie was better than anything I could have expected. It was the way she made her pastry – not too thick, not too crusty, just slightly buttery, so that it melted in the mouth. And as for the vegetables! You could almost taste the technicolour!

'Oh, Felix,' said Edith, who was glad to find something to talk to me about.

'Yes,' I said, coming out of my daydream.

'George and Sanjay have asked me to give this to you.'

'What is it?'

'A note. They wanted to apologise for their appalling

behaviour and wondered if you'd like to play cricket with them tomorrow.'

'Oh, that sounds cool. Oh, yeah. Of course, it's Sunday.'

So I headed off the following day to the school's cricket pitch. The first person I spotted was The Girl, who was amongst a small group of people who had come to watch.

'Felix!' cried out Sanjay from the pavilion. 'I didn't think you'd come.'

'What are you talking about? I like cricket,' I shouted back as I walked towards him.

'What about us though?'

'Oh. I like you too.'

'Sorry about what we did to you.'

'Don't worry. Here's my chance to take my revenge,' I said with a twinkle in my eye.

'No, it isn't. You're in my team.'

'Cool.'

'George!' shouted Sanjay.

'Yeah.'

'Bat or bowl?'

'Oh. Bat, please.'

'OK. Let's get started. Who's in first?'

'Me and Johnny.'

'OK. Get your pads on then.'

The two of them got padded and helmeted up whilst our team sorted out our positions. I had only ever played with a tennis ball at school, but I had watched many a game in the field next to my grandpa's allotment.

The day was sharp and clear and the atmosphere on the pitch was very concentrated. This was the type of quiet that I did enjoy and that very familiar hollow sound of the bat hitting the ball was really comforting. However, George and Johnny were invincible. It seemed impossible to get them out and – even worse – to stop them knocking out sixes, which they continued doing until tea time.

Despite being on the other team, I congratulated the two star players, while they were digging into iced buns and bobolate, in the pavilion.

'You weren't a pro in your previous whatsit, were you?'

'A professional what?' asked George.

'Cricketer?'

'No, I was an artist as a matter of fact.'

'What, like Picasso?'

'Not as famous as him. But then women weren't, were they?'

'Were you a woman?' I said, trying to work this one out.

'Yeah. I prefer being a bloke though, but hardly anyone here has been the same sex throughout all their lives…Anyway, let's get back to the game. I think that Johnny and I should retire. How many runs have we got so far?'

'Two hundred and fifty.'

'Oh well. Someone else can have a go.'

So they did, but they were all out pretty quickly, which meant that it was Sanjay's team's turn. I was too distracted to score anything significant though. I kept wishing that Jermaine was batting with me, as he had done so many times in the playground. But he wasn't. He was still under the spell of Mr Subaltern. These thoughts were not helping my concentration and at one point I made a real schoolboy error and got both myself and Sanjay run out.

'Well, mission accomplished,' said Sanjay.

'What do you mean?'

'You got me back.'

'Oh. I suppose I did. Sorry.'

'No, I'm the one who's sorry. I don't know what came over me the other day.'

'No, nor do I,' I said, with deliberate vagueness, as I headed off to the cliff path to go back home.

It seemed like George and Sanjay were both good people and I felt like they were almost friends now. So who had been controlling them when they were bullying me? It could have been Subaltern and he might have done it in order to provoke me into an outburst of anger so that he could get me into the palace. But why would he have wanted me there when I was just the sort of person that he clearly couldn't handle? Mild mannered individuals, like Jermaine, seemed to be far more suitable recruits.

There had to be someone else involved in all of this. Quite possibly there was a whole network, as Ivy had suggested. I would need to try and find out at school tomorrow, now that I was back in the fold again.

Just as I was thinking this, the ground beneath my feet began to vibrate. It was like being on one of those machines at the gym. I could hardly move and I had to stand still for fear of being thrown off the cliff. It was difficult to know what to do next. I needed to get home as quickly as possible. So every time the rumbling stopped, I would run as fast as I could before the whole thing started up again.

A ten-minute stroll was turning into a ten-hour marathon and if the tremors weren't enough, the wind whipped up so furiously that I found it impossible to stand upright anymore. The only option was to lie on the ground and crawl as far as I could.

All this freaky stuff was then added to by a downpour of what looked like spherical ice cubes, which pelted every part of me. It was like being endlessly slapped across the face. Not only did it hurt, but my muscles no longer seemed to work and I stopped being able to crawl as my body seized up with the cold and the pain. This must have been what it was like for my former self on that famous expedition – I thought, and for a moment I had a flashback of climbing to the top of Everest. Tenzing and my former self – Edmund Hillary – were being pounded by lumps of snow, which were dropping off the precipice. Under any other

92

circumstances, no one in their right mind would have continued any further. But with the summit so close that you could almost touch it, we had to keep going. And so did I, Felix Featherstone. Despite the cold, the seizure of my muscles and the shaking of the ground below me, I found a new energy and soldiered on until –that is – consciousness took its leave of me.

13. Infection

When I came to, I was still frozen, still wet, but the snow had melted and Old Souls' Island was calm again. I picked myself up off the ground, scratched, bruised and sore and got myself back to Mrs Higgins'.

No one appeared to be in on my return and the first thing that I did was to run myself a hot bath in order that I could warm up, but my cuts and grazes stung so much when I got into the tub that I had to resort to just dabbing myself with water instead. I then made myself a snack and some hot bobolate, went to my room and picked up *The History of Old Souls' Island* to see if there was any mention of freak weather on the island. There wasn't, but it did say that because Old Souls' World wasn't tilted like TWAWKI (The World As We Knew It), the climate remained pretty consistent throughout the year. A bit like spring in the UK. Not today, it wasn't!

It seemed more than coincidental that all this should happen just at the point that I'd had the realisation that Subaltern was definitely not acting alone – that he was amongst others. It was almost as if these people, whoever they were, could hear me thinking.

There was no doubt that something was out to get me and what I'd been through might only be the beginning. As I lay in bed that night, every creak, every rustle, every sound made me sit bolt upright and listen.

'You had us all worried last night, I can tell you,' said Mrs Higgins, as I came downstairs the following morning. 'We were wondering what on earth had happened to you when you still hadn't appeared by 7.00pm. An hour after curfew. You must have finished the cricket match by then. But then Edith suddenly thought that you might have gone to your room before we all got back. She's very wise, that girl. And sure enough, there you were…out for the count.'

'Was I?' I said, somewhat surprised. I must have slept for a bit of the night then.

'Sorry, Mrs Higgins. I was just so cold after that storm.'

'Which storm?'

'The snow storm and all the rumbling.'

'When was that?'

'Yesterday afternoon.'

'Oh. I was out getting provisions. We didn't have anything like that where I was. It must have been very localised.'

'Oh!...Mrs Higgins, do you get paid for looking after us?'

'Oh no, dear. We don't have money here.'

'What about credit cards?'

'No, no. We don't have the technology. Nothing modern anyway. Electricity generators and telephones are about as advanced as it gets here.'

'How do people buy stuff then, if there isn't any money?'

'They don't. Money doesn't make this world go round.'

'Oh. What do they do then?'

'People just get given things. Everyone on this island has a role. Either they teach at the school or they're a pupil there or else they're a landlady, a nurse, a printer, a farmer or a fisherman…'

'But how do they survive without money?'

'How do you survive **with** money? You can't use it here. Everyone gets given clothes, foods and accommodation. What would you want money for?'

'I don't know. Skateboards?'

'Oh, no. They don't allow any of that sort of nonsense.'

'Well, how come Ivy and Jo have got about four?'

'That's what we all want to know,' said Edith as she joined us in the kitchen. 'Ivy gets special privileges.'

'You don't like her, do you?' I said.

'I don't trust her, that's for sure. And she's got that fake accent.'

'What do you mean?'

'Well, she's not really American. She might have been in a previous life, but not in this one. It's just that her parents are British and she wants to disassociate herself from them. Anyway, she could get away with murder…if she was so inclined.'

'Has there ever been a murder here, Mrs Higgins?' I said, wanting to put a stop to this bit of 'Ivy bashing'.

'There's been all number of mysterious occurrences since I've been here. You're quite safe though as long as you stick to the straight and narrow. And certainly don't go near any caves. Anyway, you best get going, you two, or you'll be late for school.'

I was full of trepidation as I made my way up the tree tunnel to school. With people provoking me on one day, my records being tampered with on another and freak weather on another, what on earth was going to happen next?

I did, on the other hand, have more reason to feel better about going back to school than I ever had done. At least I'd got some friends now. So, for the first time in Assembly, I had many people to chat to before the head teacher descended the stairs and gave us our morning briefing.

'Good morning, Springers. Today, we should have been having Assembly in the big hall because, of course, today is officially the first day of term. However, we have decided to delay the collection of the second and third years, which is good news for you as it means you will receive more attention than you would normally have done in the second week. Right, if you would form an orderly line, you will follow Mrs Snapdragon as per usual.'

As I entered the Warrior classroom, Mr O'Flaherty welcomed me with open arms.

'Ah, Felix. Delighted to see you.'

'Thank you, sir.'

'Now, you won't be able to draw on all your previous lives because there is still some doubt as to what they were. So I hope you don't mind just being an observer for this session.'

'No, sir. I don't mind at all. In fact, I think that I'd be very happy.'

'Good, Felix,' said Mr O'Flaherty, who then turned to address the rest of the class. 'Can I have a volunteer?...George! That would be splendid. Please come and take your place in the grand arena.'

George positioned himself in the centre whilst Mr O'Flaherty joined the circle around him.

'So, George. Pick a life. Any life. Don't tell us what it is though. Just keep thinking about it. Now the rest of you won't know what George's catalogue of lives consisted of – apart from the last one, which was…'

I put my hand up.

'Yes, Felix.'

'An artist, sir.'

'Quite correct. But all the others, George, you have not as yet revealed to anyone…'

'No, sir.'

'Terrific, George! Now just keep thinking of that life that you picked. Think about the time you were living in, the place you were living in, what sort of clothes you were wearing, what your daily routine was.'

George had started to become very animated as he acted out who this person was.

'Ah, no, George. Don't move. Not yet. This is all about thinking. Just keep doing that. Now, does anyone here have a notion of who this person might be?'

Hands shot up all over the place. Davina said that she thought he might be an explorer – to which George nodded. Henrietta reckoned that he could have been a prisoner and Sanjay asked if he was around at the time of Queen Elizabeth the First. When George nodded to both of those, I put my hand up.

'Yes, Felix.'

'Sir Walter Raleigh. Elizabeth locked him up in the Tower of London.'

George nodded.

'Congratulations, Felix. So, we achieved this in two and a half minutes, partly by guesswork and partly by telepathy. Now, just as an experiment, I'd like Felix to stand in the centre.'

I took my place willingly.

'Now, we all know so well, from the first day in this room, who you were in your last life. But no one here, including yourself, knows who you were before Sir Edmund Hilary. This is not an exact science. It may not work but just stand still and see if another life comes to you. The one before Sir Edmund Hilary.'

I stood completely still and gave myself up to the exercise.

'Can you feel anything, Felix?'

I nodded.

'Good. Anyone got any ideas? Sanjay.'

'A soldier.'

I nodded.

'OK. Anything else?'

'A Ghurka.'

'What's a Gurkha, Sanjay? I don't think many people here will know. Or maybe we should ask Felix.'

'A Ghurka was a Nepalese soldier who fought for the Indian Army alongside the British in World War One.'

'Absolutely correct, Felix. How did you know that?'

'I didn't, sir. Not before I said it.'

'And what happened to you in World War One?'

'I got shot, sir. Killed in action in 1917.'

'Well that all fits. Edmund was born two years later. Thank you very much, Felix.'

As Mr O'Flaherty had wanted to congratulate me on the session, I was the last to leave the Warriors Room at break time. Wandering along the corridor on my own, I realised that someone **must** have interfered with my records if, that is, my life before Sir Edmund had been as honourable as it seems it must have been.

Maybe Mr Subaltern had played around with the details of my past lives if he'd wanted me to become part of his palace community. When that hadn't worked, he had had to resort to something else – provoke me to use physical violence in the school. That bit added up, but it couldn't have been him that was responsible for that freak storm. If he wasn't able to have control over my anger, he definitely couldn't control the weather.

My thoughts were interrupted however by a visit from my multi-coloured dragonfly friend. Long time, no see – or at least that's what it felt like after my recent ordeal. It did its usual somersault in response before leading me towards the sanatorium. I wasn't ill or injured, but I thought that I better follow it. As I got to the door though, I stopped and turned to go back the way I had just come from. But the dragonfly caught up with me and proceeded to dive bomb me, as if to tell me that I must go back and knock on the door. Leaving me with no other option, I did as instructed.

'Hello, Felix,' said the matron. 'Don't tell me that you've come down with it as well.'

'What's that, miss?'

'This bug that all the collectors have got.'

'Oh, no,' I said, peering in to see Adrian and nine others flat out on their beds. The two boys with the stretched arms and legs were there as well, but their limbs seemed to have shrunk back to the right size and they were both up and about again. They had no choice, of course. All the other beds were more urgently required.

'That's a relief. Well, what can I help you with?'

'Oh, I just wanted you to check my hand from that bite that I got the other day.'

'It looks like it's healed very nicely, Felix.'

'Thank you, miss. I won't bother you then.'

I looked up to thank my friend for showing me all this, but the dragonfly had flown off to do something else.

What was going on? Something even stranger than anything that I had experienced so far. Most of the collectors, except for Jo, had been struck down with a bug. This was too much of a coincidence. We'd been informed that the second years were not coming back when they should have done. This must be the reason. But why had no one just come clean about it?

I had to let Jo know about this immediately. So I rushed down to the cottage as soon as school was over and knocked heavily on the door.

'Can I come in?' I said, as soon as Jo appeared.

'Yeah. Of course, man.'

'Have you seen any of your collector friends recently?'

'Oh, no. I haven't been out much.'

'Well, I have and they're not well.'

'Aren't they?'

'No. They're all in the sanatorium and they've come down with a really serious bug. That's why the second years aren't back.'

'Yeah. Of course.'

'Although, come to think of it, why haven't you brought any?'

'Oh…um…I was told not to bother until next week,' said Jo, a little vaguely.

'Oh, so you knew already?'

'Only that, man. I didn't know it was because my colleagues were ill. No!'

'All I can say is that you were right about it being a whole network of people.'

'What, the collectors?'

'No, whatever is causing all these weird things to happen. It can't be Mr Subaltern on his own. He can't control me, let alone the forces of nature. But who is it that he's in league with?'

'I don't know,' said Ivy as she came down the stairs to join them. 'But it's for you to find out. You're at school all day. You can be our spy in the camp. I'm sure that more will be revealed.'

'Perhaps I should go back and ask the collectors themselves.'

'No. That's not a good idea. They won't tell you anyway. They'll be terrified that whoever is responsible will make them even worse. They won't reveal anything. Just keep your eyes open. That's all.'

'Very well,' I said, as I walked over to the front door. 'I'll keep you updated. See you.'

Quite possibly, the collectors would be too frightened to reveal who was behind their illness. But I wasn't going to let that stop me from finding out a bit more. I needed to have an excuse to return to the sanatorium and went up the tree tunnel, looking out to see if there were any Janus-facers around.

I was in luck. One was wandering straight towards me. I stopped still, so as not to frighten it away and then let the thing approach me.

'Hello, little fellow,' I said as I gave it a stroke. True to form, it turned over on to its back and I started rubbing its tummy. The animal was clearly enjoying this immensely and I was waiting, with a bit of anxiety, for it to turn on me.

'I wouldn't do that if I were you,' called out a voice from further up the tree tunnel. 'They bite.'

'Oh. Hi, Sanjay. Thanks. No I've been caught out before with these things. But this one seems to be OK.'

'You won't know until it's gone for you.'

'True!'

'Where are you off to, Felix? Curfew's in a few minutes.'

'Just going back to school to get something.'

'Oh. OK. See you tomorrow then.'

The Janus-facer had now disappeared. How annoying. I hadn't managed to get myself bitten. I needed to injure myself somehow though. I picked up a branch and tried to scratch my arm, but all it did was to make a red mark. So I decided just to keep walking and hope that something would show up. As I approached the school gates, I still couldn't see anything that I could use, except the milk bottles that had been left outside for the milkman.

I quickly picked one up and then took it back down the tunnel where I smashed it against a tree. I then took one of the shards of glass and ran it down my knee until I'd made a decent cut. As I hurried back to the school though, I realised that I'd probably done too good a job. Blood was pouring all over the place.

I rang the bell and waited for the janitor to appear.

'Sorry to bother you, but I fell over onto some glass in the tree tunnel, on my way back home.'

'What was glass doing in the tree tunnel?' said the janitor suspiciously.

'I don't know.'

'You better come in. You know where the sanatorium is?'

'Yes. I do.'

'Well, you better be quick. Otherwise there won't be any of that stuff left in your body.'

'No. You're right. Thank you.'

After knocking on the door of the sanatorium, I looked back to see the janitor mopping up the river of blood that I'd spilt all the way down the corridor.

'Felix, what brings you here at this hour? Not another bite from a Janus-facer?' said the matron jokingly.

Thank god I hadn't allowed that to happen. It would have been far too obvious.

'No, I fell over onto some glass in the tree tunnel.'

'Now, what would broken glass be doing in the tree tunnel?'

'I don't know, miss.'

'Never mind. Let's get you bandaged up. Come in and sit down where you can find a space. We're full to bursting here at the moment. And hold this against your knee,' she said, handing me a wet cloth.

I did so and then quickly looked to see if I could find Adrian. It was difficult to work out who everyone was, as most of them were buried under their blankets. There was however a seat next to the bed that I'd seen Adrian on earlier.

'Evening, Felix,' said a voice from underneath the covers.

'How did you know it was me?' I whispered, keeping my distance so as not to get infected.

'Well, if I can't recognise your voice by now, there's something very wrong with me.'

'There is something very wrong with you, isn't there?'

'Yes, there is. It's not good at all.'

'How come it's only the collectors that have got it?'

'That's what we all want to know,' whispered Adrian. 'But I have a pretty good idea who might be behind all of this.'

'Felix Featherstone,' called out the matron.

'Yes, miss.'

'You are not to disturb any of my patients,' she said in a voice completely different from her jovial, friendly one.

'Oh, I'm sorry, miss,' I said, as I hobbled over to her desk.

'Now let's get this sorted out. Good, there doesn't appear to be any glass lodged in your knee. You can't have fallen too hard on it.'

'No, I didn't, miss.'

'Good. I can put a bandage on now then,' she said, after she'd finished washing it down.

'Thank you, miss,' I said, as she dressed the wound.

'Well, that will be all. Off you go!'

'Thank you, miss.'

But there was no answer. She was not happy with me. Why had she been so weird with me and stopped me from talking to the collectors? If anything was going to disturb them, it would be her voice booming across the room at me.

Although I had gone against their advice, I still felt that I needed to tell Ivy and Jo about what had happened in the sanatorium. So I went back down to the cottage to see them again.

'Back again already? Don't tell me you've got some news,' said Ivy as she opened the door.

'I have actually. It may be urgent too, as it could affect Jo.'

'Oh!'

'I know that you didn't think that it was a good idea, but I went to the sanatorium.'

'You must have done something before that,' she said, looking down at the blood on my trousers.

'Yes, I cut myself on some glass.'

'How convenient!'

'Well, I did it deliberately.'

'I'd never have guessed,' she said sarcastically. 'So that you had an excuse to see Matron?'

'Yes.'

'And what did she say?'

'Well, it wasn't what she said. It was what my collector said that was...'

'What did he say then?'

'He just said that it was too coincidental that all the collectors had gone down with this whatever-it-is and he thought that he knew who was behind it.'

'Really?'

'Yes.'

'And who might that be?' enquired Ivy.

'I don't know. He didn't have a chance to tell me. It might be that nice matron though because she suddenly turned all funny.'

'Maybe!'

'Anyway, I thought I better warn Jo. Just in case anyone tries to do something to him.'

'That's most thoughtful, Felix.'

'I better get back. Curfew's been and gone.'

'Look after that leg,' she said, putting her hand gently on the bandage. 'These things can get infected.'

When I got back to Mrs Higgins', I didn't want to talk to anyone. So I sneaked up the stairs to my bedroom. As I sat down on a chair, I suddenly became aware of a sharp tingling sensation in my knee. Maybe Ivy was right. It could have got infected.

14. Judgements

The next morning, I woke up in agony. My leg had puffed up out of all proportion and I couldn't get out of bed.

'Felix,' called Mrs Higgins at eight o'clock. 'Time to get up.'

'I can't get up, Mrs Higgins. My leg looks like an elephant's.'

A few days in bed was all that Mrs H could suggest, which meant that another excuse to drop into the sanatorium was out of the question. Maybe the matron had deliberately infected my leg for that very reason. When I finally did get better and returned to school though, I made it my mission to go and speak to her before doing anything else.

'Come in,' she said, as I knocked on her door.

'Thank you,' I said.

'I'm sorry that I wasn't able to come down to you. I've been rushed off my feet with this bug that all the collectors have gone down with.'

I looked through the office door into the sick room and saw that it was empty.

'But there's no one here. Does that mean that they're all better now?'

'No. Sadly not,' she said as she started to remove my bandage. 'We had to move them to another site to ensure that whatever it is that they've got doesn't spread round the rest of the school.'

'What is it they have got?'

'No one knows. It's a bit of a mystery. They could probably diagnose it in TWAWKI, but we don't have either the knowledge or the equipment that they have there.'

'Oh.'

'Anyway, your leg has gone down to its normal size and it doesn't look as if it's infected anymore. We'll leave the bandage off for now so that it can breathe.'

'So what was wrong with it?'

'I don't know. Another little mystery.'

'Matron!'

'Yes, Felix.'

'Do you think that it's a coincidence that the only people who got the bug were collectors?'

'Now, Felix, do you really think that that hadn't crossed my mind?'

'Of course not.'

'The last thing we need here is a scare but, between you and me, there is something deeply sinister going on.'

'That's the word I keep thinking of.'

'Is it, Felix? Well, keep it to yourself.'

'I will, Matron. Thank you.'

I went back down the corridor and into the hall where Assembly was about to begin.

'Good morning, Springers,' said the head teacher in his customary welcoming manner. 'And we are all still Springers. Unfortunately, the second and third years still can't be with us as we're a bit short of collectors at the moment. They've all gone down with the flu.'

This was not what Matron had said and whatever it was seemed a lot worse than flu. Was this some kind of cover up?

'Be not afeard,' he quickly added. 'They're all on another site now. So there's no risk of contagion. This does mean though that you will continue to get special attention as all the guides are here exclusively at your service. Now, instead of attaching you to any particular one today, we're going to give you the freedom to choose who you want to have a one-to-one session with. It's a bit of a free for all, but we can't allow chaos. So what I'm going to ask Mrs Pettifer to do is to call your names out one by one and then it'll be a matter of 'first come, first served'. If you want to see a guide who's already busy, you are very welcome to wait outside their room. In some cases, you will need to form an orderly queue.'

This was perfect. Although I desperately wanted to track Adrian down and find out who he had been talking about, I might be able to do a bit of detective work myself by talking to some of the staff. As I looked up at the gallery and waited for my name to be called out, I could see that Asha and Mr O'Flaherty had both already attracted big, long queues. But I didn't need to speak to either of them as I'd already had as much out of them as I could for the moment. The best people to talk to would probably be the ones who nobody wanted to see. The unpopular ones in other words.

When my name was called out, I walked up the stairs to the gallery and casually wandered along it. I was secretly hoping that my dragonfly friend might suddenly appear and lead me to a room where I might glean some important information, but it didn't. So I let my instinct guide me instead and knocked on the first door that took my fancy.

'Come in,' said a very distinctive voice.

'Thank you,' I said, as I saw that its owner was as precise and particular as he sounded.

'Good morning, Felix. My name's Mr Advocate. How's it all been going since you left the palace?'

'Oh. It's good. I've made friends with George and Sanjay, who were the…'

'Yes, I know what you're trying to say. Good, I'm glad to hear it. So order has been restored in your life, has it?'

'Well, not exactly.'

'Please. Tell me. That's what I'm here for.'

'Well, it's nothing really. Just some strange things…'

'Strange things are not nothing, Felix.'

'No.'

'Well, what are these strange things?'

'I can't really say.'

'Or rather, you mean you don't **want** to say.'

'Yes.'

'Come on, Felix. You can trust me.'

'When I came back from playing cricket the other day, I got caught in a big storm,' I said, thinking it might be worth trying to see how Mr Advocate reacted.

'A storm? What kind of storm?'

'I got bombarded with ice pellets.'

'Where was this?'

'At the beginning of the path that leads to the cricket pitch.'

'Interesting,' he said dubiously. 'Anyone else experience this?'

'I don't think so, sir. But I just wanted to know whether this was normal.'

'No. It's not normal at all. It is as strange as you have just described it. Anything else?'

'Well, I still don't know why George and Sanjay behaved the

way they did.'

'Boys will be boys, Felix. It's universal. That type of behaviour. Anything else?'

'Yes. The collectors. It seems a bit of a …'

'Coincidence? Not really. They were all staying in the same accommodation, the Old Barn, that's all. The only one that didn't get it was Jo, because he was at the cottage. Anything else?'

'My records have been changed.'

'We don't have any real proof of that yet.'

'Apart from what happened in Mr O'Flaherty's class the other day.'

'Yes, I heard about that. Just because you came up with someone – a Gurkha, wasn't it – it doesn't **prove** anything. In fact, as far as I understand it, someone else suggested it and you agreed.'

'Maybe. But the big thing is that Stonehenge was pink the other day.'

'Yes, that's what Mrs Butcher said.'

'Yes, but that was on another occasion,' I said, almost knowing what was coming next.

'Well, whenever it was, her husband said that she was imagining things. Are you sure that you weren't? It could just have been the light from the sol setting.'

'I don't know, sir.'

'No, nor do I. I don't know what to say, Felix. You've presented me with a whole list of things that are going on around you, which could, on the one hand, be deeply sinister…'

'Yes, that's the word I would use.'

'…but on the other, have a perfectly rational explanation.'

'Apart from the…'

'Apart from the storm, which only you were party to. Do you see what I'm driving at? In a court of law, I don't think your jury would be convinced. Sorry, Felix. This is not what you wanted

110

to hear, is it? However, at least you can put your mind at rest. Things are not nearly as **sinister** as you are imagining. In fact, they're probably not sinister at all.'

'Thank you, sir,' I said, as Mr Advocate got up to shake my hand.

'Thank you, Felix. Stop worrying and go off and enjoy yourself. That's what you're here for.'

I walked out of the room as calmly as possible, down the corridor to the staircase and then, when no one appeared to be looking, kicked one of the bannisters.

'Felix!' called out Edith, as she was coming out of one of the rooms.

'Oh. Hi, Edith.'

'So, who's been winding you up?'

'Mr Advocate. He didn't believe anything I was telling him.'

'Oh, yes. He likes to present the counter argument.'

'It's so unfair.'

'Remember who else you are in this world. You don't always have to react like Felix.'

'But he's wrong.'

'I'm sure he is, but instead of kicking the bannister, why don't you try and do something useful with your position?'

'Like what?'

'Find a way of proving that you were right. Anyway, it looks like your friend wants you.'

I looked up to see the dragonfly, who performed his usual somersault before leading me out of the school's doors, through the tree tunnel and in the direction of the canal. What was the point of going back to the Venetian palace? There was no way that I was going to persuade Jermaine to leave. So I walked the other way towards Mrs Higgins'. The dragonfly was having none of this though and kept coming back to hover over my head and then start flying off in the other direction. The more I ignored it, the closer it got to my face and the more of of a pest it became, flapping its wings right next to my left ear.

So I gave in eventually and did what it so clearly wanted me to. Maybe Subaltern would be having a meeting with some of his fellow collaborators. But it was getting dark and the ferryman would have knocked off for the day. I wouldn't be able to get to the palace. As I approached the canal however, I realised that this must be the point. There was no one around. I'd do what I had suggested to Jermaine. Swim! For what purpose, I had no idea, but the dragonfly seemed insistent that I did. I looked up at my friend as if to tell him that I'd understood. The dragonfly did a somersault to acknowledge that and then started knocking against my shirt.

'Take this off?' I said.

Another somersault. So I did. The dragonfly then swooped down and knocked against first my trousers and then my shoes. Message received and understood.

'Strip down to your underpants, in other words,' I said.

I then took the plunge, but this was not as easy as I had imagined. As I dived in, I could taste the muddiness of the water and feel its silt against my eyes. I grabbed my clothes and held them up in the air as I swam towards the palace.

As I got close to it, the front door suddenly opened. Mr Subaltern came out and had a look around him. Although it was nearly dark, the moons were as full as they had been a few nights before. I quickly put my clothes down behind a pillar and then held my nose and submerged myself under water. I'd done this at school. My record was 95 seconds. Unable to stay under for any longer, I came up for air. Mr Subaltern was still there and took a look in my direction. I snatched a quick breath and went straight back under again. When I re-emerged the next time, I could see that Mr Subaltern was looking the other way. The dragonfly was distracting him – perhaps too much though, as he was attempting to swat it with his copy of Old Souls' Times.

This was desperate. At the moment, this insect was the best friend I had on Old Souls' Island. I picked up a stone from the bank of the canal and flung it as far as I could to distract him and then went under the water again. This was killing me. I couldn't do any more of these. Fortunately, as I came up, I heard Jermaine's voice.

'Excuse me, sir.'

'Yes, Jermaine.'

'I think I'm ready.'

'Oh. Jolly good. Let's go into my office.'

This sounded worse than ever. As soon as they were inside, I swam up to the palace and climbed up through one of the arches. I grabbed hold of my clothes, did a quick dry down with my shirt, got dressed and then went up to the front door. I was about to knock on it when 'Mr Dragonfly' started flapping his wings in an agitated manner. Of course! No one was going to let me in without a whole list of questions and I certainly wouldn't be able to eavesdrop on the conversation between Mr Subaltern and Jermaine. The only way that I could do that was if I climbed up the front of the building. All of its carvings, statues and protrusions gave me enough things to hold onto or to use as footings. So I proceeded to make my way up the wall.

'So you think you're ready to talk?' I heard Mr Subaltern say, just as I'd positioned myself alongside the office window.

'Yes, sir,' answered Jermaine.

'Very well. Have you rehearsed what you are going to say?'

'No, but all I do know is that I'm prepared to say whatever comes into my head. I'm no longer afraid of the truth.'

'Off you go then.'

'I am in a Second World War plane. A Spitfire. Flying high above the clouds.'

Jermaine's voice suddenly became like the posh one he used when he was mucking around. Only this time, he wasn't joking. He was for real.

113

'It feels like another world and my best friends are up here too, flying in formation either side of me. There is no one down below on Earth who could possibly be a better friend. No one else understands how exhilarating it is, after sitting around playing chess for ten hours and then suddenly getting the call for you to scramble…to run as fast as you can towards your plane and take it up into the air in seconds. No one else understands how it feels to be in a plane on your own – a sitting target. And no one else understands what it is like to lose your best friend when you are in this other world.'

This hit home with me in more ways than one.

'Carry on,' said Mr Subaltern.

'We suddenly find ourselves head on with an oncoming fleet of Messerschmitts. We exchange fire, but five of my chaps are hit and twirl down through the clouds…and into the sea. I knock down as many of the other side as possible and then fly back to base – a sole survivor.'

Despite the tragic circumstances that Jermaine was describing, this was music to my ears. My friend had been a hero – just like I had been. Not a villain, not a murderer.

'Back on the ground, the dispersal hut is empty but it's crowded with ghosts. I may have been lucky to have survived, but at that moment I wish so desperately that I hadn't. How can I still have life when my best friends haven't? What right do I have to still be here?'

'Good, Jermaine. Now move forward in time to after the war. Maybe with your family.'

'Oh, I can see it. It's 1960 and I'm sitting down to dinner with my family and my son asks me what I did during the war. I look at him quizzically and say: "I think it's time for you to go to bed, isn't it?"…'

'What does he say?' interjected Mr Subaltern.

There was a silence and I was not sure whether I could hold on any longer. I was about to ease myself down as my hands were losing their grip. But I needed to hear this. I took my right hand off the masonry, which it was clinging to, and flexed it back and forward until it had renewed strength and then did the same with the other hand.

'Oh, well. He doesn't want to go to bed,' said Jermaine.

'And how do you react to that?'

'I don't. I've closed up. I don't say anything.'

'How are you feeling now?'

'Can we change the subject, please?'

'We will indeed. Well done, Jermaine. You've got there. You've done it.'

'Thank you, sir.'

At that moment, one of my footings broke off and I was no longer able to keep a grip. There was no other option than to let myself drop and I plummeted into the water with a huge splash. It was bad enough trying to swim in this murky water, but dropping down below the surface was like falling into a black hole. I couldn't come back up for air though for fear of being seen. They must have heard me inside. So I swam as far as I could underwater without opening my eyes, nostrils or lips. The narrowness and straightness of the canal were the only thing which gave me confidence that I was heading in the right direction. As I emerged, I continued swimming as fast as possible to the end. I then climbed out of the water, looking like some weirdo creature emerging from a lagoon, and ran back along the cliff path with difficulty. Not only were my clothes completely drenched, but they were also covered in mud and all sorts of slimy vegetation.

Once I had made some ground, I looked back to see if anyone from the palace had come out to investigate. No sign from any of them, but The Girl was following me. Again!

She was behaving in the same way as before and was pretending to mind her own business, picking a few flowers in the moonlight and then smelling them. At least whatever she was doing seemed quite innocent though. She had a friendly and caring quality about her, but did she really imagine that she wasn't acting suspiciously?

I nearly turned back to go and confront her, but I had to go and tell Ivy and Jo all about this new discovery. I did check behind me a few times though and could still see her in the distance when I knocked on Ivy's door.

I was greeted by Jo, who was as friendly as ever, but very low-key.

'Hi, man. How y' doin? What's going down? Hey, you're all wet, man.'

'Yeah, I know but it was worth it. I think I might have made a bit of a discovery. Mr Subaltern's not the monster that we thought he was.'

'No?'

'No. Definitely not! He's just helped Jermaine to find his previous self. I heard it all.'

'You've got a few things to learn, young Felix,' Ivy intervened. 'The devil plays devious games and you've just fallen for one.'

'Are you sure?'

'Yes, of course. Some other problem will mysteriously appear for Jermaine and there'll be a new diagnosis, which will mean that he'll never get out. Ever!'

'Really?'

'Yes. I should know. I've been in there myself.'

'But you got out!'

'Yes. Only because I worked out how to play the man at his own game. Believe you me, the man is evil. There's no two ways about it. We just need to work out who else he's working with. Don't be fooled by anyone here.'

'No, I won't.'

'Well, let us know when you have any leads.'

'I will.'

'Oh. And Felix!'

'Yes.'

'Take this,' she said, handing me a small silvery stone.

'What is it?'

'It's for good luck. You need it at the moment. Keep it in your pocket.'

'OK.'

15. Possession

The next day, after Assembly, our class was taken to the Exhibition Room, which looked like a gigantic greenhouse, where Mr O'Flaherty had laid out a whole range of artefacts that had some relevance to our past lives. This included a length of rope that was used on the Everest expedition.

'Now today, we have a little treat in store. Something to stimulate the mind, the spirit, not to mention the soul. I'm going to let you have a wander and have a look at all these precious items before we discuss their relevance. You are all, of course, very trustworthy but I will impress upon you that not only are they very precious but we have gone to great lengths to obtain these items since we discovered who you all were. Some of our collectors made special trips back to TWAWKI – before they got ill, that is – in order to secure them. All righty. Off you go,

Ladies and Gentlemen!'

I picked up a floral hat that was in front of me, took a quick look and then put it down again. I then moved on to look at a 1940s telephone, made out of Bakelite plastic, and picked up its receiver.

'Mayfair 142,' I said in my silly posh accent. 'Who do you wish to…?' I continued until I felt something being put onto my head. I looked round to see Sanjay laughing.

'Suits you,' said Sanjay.

I took the hat off and saw that it was the floral one. Under normal circumstances I would have found this funny, but today I was furious. I threw it across the room to Sanjay and shouted:

'Not as much as it would you. Put it on!'

'OK,' said Sanjay and did as had been requested.

I then picked up a dress and threw that over to Sanjay.

'And why not try this one on for size, Sweetheart!' I said mockingly.

Sanjay picked it up and held it up to himself. Everyone laughed uproariously.

'Oh. So you think that's funny, do you? How about this then?'

I went up to the table, picked up one end of it and allowed glass bowls, delicate wooden boxes and everything else to go crashing onto the floor and break into little pieces.

The whole room went silent and Mr O'Flaherty intervened.

'Felix Featherstone! Are you aware of what you have just done?'

'Yes, I've just knocked over a table at a jumble sale. So what?'

'As I said at the beginning of the lesson, these items…'

'…are complete and utter garbage,' I cut in.

'I think that we've perhaps gone a bit too far, Felix. Have you forgotten what noble people you were in your past lives?'

'Do you really think that I believe in all that RUBBISH?'

'Come here, Felix.'

'No, you come here!' I shouted. A small part of me was looking down on myself in astonishment that I could be so rude. I'd never gone this far before. But the rest of me was so consumed with rage and anger that this outburst was absolutely impossible to control.

'I'm warning you, Felix.'

'And I'm warning you. Don't mess with me. I'm in a bad mood today.'

'All right,' said Mr O'Flaherty. 'We won't mess with you, but you will be taking yourself to see the head teacher right now. You can explain to him…'

'I'm not taking myself.'

'Very well. In that case, **we** will take you.'

'Who's we?'

'Me, for a start,' replied Mr O'Flaherty, who was now showing a side of himself that none of us had ever seen before.

'Come on then. Try it. You see if you can take me.'

'Grab him, Warriors,' cried out Mr O'Flaherty and a couple of the bravest boys got hold of either arm. This was not enough though. I threw them off in seconds.

'And again!' shouted Mr O'Flaherty. This time, three boys and three girls got hold of me. I was now kicking and screaming. Four of them had a limb each, whilst the other two held onto my torso. They then marched me down the corridor to the head's office.

'Don't worry about that. We'll go straight to the Venetian palace.'

Not for one second did I give up the struggle as the group carried me down through the tree tunnel, along the cliff path and up to the canal.

The ferryman used some of his rope to restrain me before putting me into the gondola. The journey down the canal was even slower than last time and I lay on the floor of the boat, kicking against the sides of it.

Mr O'Flaherty's helpers then carried me through the front door of the palace and over the Bridge of Sighs, which should on this occasion have been renamed the Bridge of Screams. They then took me down to the ancient old cells on the ground floor and handcuffed me to a chain on the wall.

'Let's leave him to cool off,' said Mr O'Flaherty as he ushered the pupils out and shut the door behind him.

A shaft of light, which beamed through the cell's tiny window, was only just strong enough for me to be able to make out the jagged stone walls and uneven concrete floor, which was both damp and smelly. In my state of complete exhaustion, I had no option other than to sit down on it though. Why had I got so angry? It was all about a stupid dress. I'd worked so hard to make a new group of friends and now, in one single moment, I'd fallen out with all of them. I was definitely my own worst enemy. Forget about everyone else.

I'd gone too far. I'd turned over tables before, but then shocked myself into stopping. I'd never taken on a teacher. Lying down on the floor in despair, I vowed to myself that I was going to stop having these tantrums once and for all.

Some minutes later, I suddenly became aware of a flapping noise coming from the corner of the cell. A tiny bird, a fledgling, was trying to get itself up off the floor. Once it was on its feet, it made an attempt to fly into the air. But each time it did so, it would end up falling onto the hard concrete and hurting itself. This did not stop it from keeping on trying however. I counted its number of attempts until eventually, on the eighth, it was finally properly in flight and swooping around the cell with great delight.

It then headed towards the window and perched itself in between a couple of the bars. As there was no glass, it was able from there to head off into the open sky. I watched with envy as this little creature found its freedom. Life is a challenge for everything, I thought. Not just for people.

My reverie was interrupted, however, by the sound of a key turning in the door. It was Mr Subaltern.

'So, Felix,' he said in his high pitched voice. 'You've had a bit of a time, I hear.'

'Yes.'

'Now, I'm going to unlock your handcuffs, so that you will be free to walk around the room,' he said in his measured way. 'But the door is locked from the outside, so you won't be able to get out.'

'Oh,' I muttered, as he released me from the chains, and then just stood still
and stared at the floor.

'Look at me, Felix,' continued Mr Subaltern. 'You're not a bad kid, but you do, as we both know, still have a severe problem with your anger issues.'

'Yes, sir.'

'Why do you think this is?'

'I don't know, but people...'

'Psychiatrists?'

'Yes, psychiatrists think that it's something to do with my mother dying on my third birthday, sir.'

'Why does that make you angry, Felix?'

'Because it was my fault.'

Mr Subaltern saw that I was trying to hold back the tears and he changed his tone completely.

'Why was it your fault?' he said as sympathetically as he could.

'If I hadn't been born, she wouldn't have died.'

'No, no. That is not your fault, Felix.'

I couldn't answer. The tears were beginning to drop.

'Now, Felix. I'd love to say that we could let you back into the palace itself. However, we are not able to take that risk. I'm sorry to say that you are still a liability. If you flipped again, you could do some damage. But I will get the staff here to provide you with whatever food that you desire.'

'Thank you, sir.'

'I can see that you are no longer showing signs of volatility. So I think perhaps that we can allow you to have some visitors. There will be **someone** outside the door however, just in case anything should happen. Do you understand?'

'Yes, sir.'

'Edith, you may come in,' he called out.

The door was unlocked and Edith came straight over to me and put her arms around me.

'I'll leave you to it then,' said Mr Subaltern as he went out, closing the door behind him.

'Are you OK now?' she said.

'I don't know. I don't really understand what's going on,' I replied.

'I do.'

'Do you?'

'Yes. You were possessed. There's no doubt about it. Just like George and Sanjay were. Someone or something was taking full advantage of your fiery temper.'

'Do you think so?'

'I know so. Someone is trying to manipulate you and we have to find out who it is. In the meantime, you have another visitor who may be able to help you.'

'Who's that?'

'The Girl!'

'Oh!'

'Can I ask her to come in?'

'OK.'

She opened the door and The Girl came in.

'Hello, Felix. I'm Chantelle.'

'Hi, Chantelle. I've seen you around,' I said teasingly.

'Yes, yes. You have,' said Chantelle. 'I'm sorry. Now this might sound a bit strange but...'

'Just a minute, Chantelle,' Edith said, interrupting. 'I think that we should get Mr Subaltern in to witness this.'

'Yes, good idea.'

Edith opened the door and called out for him.

'Yes?' he said, as he came back into the room. 'You want me to ...'

'...to listen to this. Yes, please, Mr Subaltern.'

'Yes, I think that I should,' he replied.

'I was just going to say that I know this might sound a bit strange but...'

'Yes, Chantelle. Keep going,' said Mr Subaltern.

'I am...I was your mother, Felix. Judy Featherstone.'

I looked at her with disbelief.

'Yes, I was and – now I know that – I find it very difficult not to keep looking at you and making sure that you're OK.'

'Oh, I see. How long have you known?'

'I found out on the first day. And I want you to know that I'm very happy to meet you. I also want to tell you that I'm very happy in my life. Judy Featherstone is now Chantelle Williams and she is...I am...very happy. So you have to stop feeling guilty.'

What had started as droplets now turned into an endless stream from my eyes. I was no longer able to talk.

Edith turned to Mr Subaltern.

'Do you think that this boy is going to have another one of his tantrums now?'

'No, I don't. Take him back to Mrs Higgins'.'

'Thank you,' said Edith.

'But, Edith,' he said as she escorted me out of the room.

'Yes, sir.'

'We still can't allow him back to school. Not until the shock of today has died down and we can be more certain about his records. In the meantime, Felix, you better get yourself up to the bathroom and we'll get you a change of clothes. It stinks in here.'

16. Home Truths

As it was dark on the way home and the moons were hidden by clouds, it was impossible to see what colour Stonehenge was. That was probably all for the good though as tonight was not a night for more distress. It was a night for celebration. And that's what we got. When we opened the front door of Mrs Higgins', the smell of roast something-or-other wafted through the air.

'Now don't go thinking that I do this every night. But this one is a special one. You're back to school next week as is young Master Jermaine, who's upstairs unpacking as we speak. He told me that you were on your way.'

'Is he?' I said, realising that Ivy and Jo had been totally wrong about him staying there forever and about Mr Subaltern, of course.

'He arrived about an hour ago. So everything's…'

'Mrs Higgins,' I interrupted. 'Sorry to stop you there, but can we please still have the roast. It's just that…'

'What on earth do you think I've just cooked it for?'

'It's just that I don't know if I'm going back to school next week.'

'Yes, you are,' said Mrs Higgins. 'They've got the original copies of your records. One of your fellow pupils found them in the woods, just next to the tree tunnel. They're letting you go back in a few days' time.'

'Really!' I said and would have asked for more details had I not been distracted by the sight of my friend walking down the stairs. 'Jermaine! This is amazing. Suddenly everything seems to be turning out OK again.'

'We've all missed you,' said Mrs Higgins. 'Now let's sit down and dig into the roast to celebrate.'

'If I'd known this was going to happen, I'd have made a cake as well,' said Edith.

'Do you think that I hadn't thought of that? Well, we haven't got a cake, but we do have Mrs Higgins' Dreamy Pudding, *la specialite de la maison.*'

'What's that in English?' asked Jermaine.

'The speciality of the house. It's legendary right across this island.'

'Hurrah!' we all shouted in unison, with a jubilation that made us now realise how happy we were once again.

The roast dinner lived up to all our expectations. The vegetables had that deliciously crispy exterior and a tang of wood smoke permeating through them.

'I'd like to propose a toast,' I said, 'to the beginning of a new chapter, here on Old Souls' Island.' For tonight, at least, we could forget about the dark side of this strange place.

'Yeah, man!' agreed Jermaine. 'We've survived the hard times. Now it's the fun times.'

127

'Well, we can certainly do that now that we all know who we are – or rather were,' I said.

'Yes,' said Jermaine, who then went on to tell us about his revelation and explained that the reason that it had been so difficult to return to his previous self was because that person had been so tormented for most of his life and had never been able to get over the loss of so many of his friends. He'd also suffered from survivor's guilt and found it difficult to continue going on living when so many of his best friends were dead.

'So how come you've never had a problem flying fighter jets around the park then?' I asked.

'Flying fighter jets round the park?' exclaimed Mrs Higgins. 'Well, I ask you. What do they let youngsters get up to on TWAWKI these days?'

'Oh, no. It was only pretending, Mrs Higgins.'

'I suppose I was sort of enjoying the thrill of it all…'

'…without realising its significance,' said Edith finishing his sentence.

'And it's only now that you know the full story,' I concluded.

'Yes, I guess I won't want to be doing that for a while.'

'Anyway, let's not dwell on all that,' said Mrs Higgins. 'Who wants a bit of Dreamy Pudding?'

'Yes, please,' we all responded in unison.

'Felix?' said Edith, as Mrs Higgins was serving up.

'Yes, Edith.'

'I quite fancy meeting your friend, Ivy.'

'Oh. Are you still seeing her, bruv?' said Jermaine, cheekily.

'Do you?' I said to Edith, ignoring Jermaine's remark. 'I thought you didn't like her.'

'Well, I'll only find out what I really think of her if I get to know her.'

'Well, I don't think that I'll be going down there for a few days.'

'Really?'

'No, but I suppose you could go there and pretend that you were looking for me. If you really want to.'

'OK. I might do that then.'

Having just had the day I'd had and Dreamy Pudding on top of it, I was beginning to feel sleepy. So I went up to my room, lay down on my bed and began to doze off. I was suddenly awoken however by a visit from my friend – the dragonfly.

'What is this?' I blurted out as I came to. 'Oh it's you. Hello. Thank you for everything you did this afternoon. You don't want me to go somewhere else, do you?'

The dragonfly did one of his somersaults.

'Now?' I exclaimed.

It did a repeat.

'Are you quite sure? I'm knackered.'

It now went into a continuous rolling somersault.

'OK,' I said wearily and got up out of my bed.

'I suppose I need to get dressed now, do I?'

The somersault just kept on going.

When I was ready, my friend – as always – led the way. I crept down the stairs and out of the front door. After a few minutes of walking though, I came to a sudden stop.

'Hang on,' I said, when I'd worked out that it was leading me to Ivy and Jo's. 'I really don't want to go down there at the moment.'

This sent my multi-coloured friend into a frenzy. He repeated the same action over and over again, flying forward a few feet and then coming back to get me, until eventually I gave in.

As we reached the house, instead of leading me to the front door, the dragonfly behaved in the same way as he had at the Venetian palace. I understood what to do and crouched down underneath one of the windows. I could hear Ivy talking to someone.

'Oh, yes. So you're the one that's sharing a house with Felix and Jermaine.'

Had Edith gone down there already?

'Yes, I am and I was beginning to feel a bit left out as they've both hung out with you, and I haven't.'

'Why, is this supposed to be a cool place or something?' said Ivy, sounding a bit more innocent than she usually did.

'Yes, of course. You're the only pupil who seems to have their own house. It's amazing!'

'It really is, isn't it!'

'You know, I might be totally wrong about this, but I feel that you could be someone who thinks a bit like I do. A sort of kindred spirit.'

'Really?'

'Yeah, I do. In fact, that's what I felt when I met you the last time I was here. And I wanted to talk to you about that.'

'What's there to talk about exactly?' said Ivy suspiciously.

'Let's put it this way. I've only been here a few days, but I don't think that I could stay here any longer without…how shall I say it?…changing a few things.'

'What? The way the school is run. Things like that?'

'No, no. Much more than that. Now, you may want to report me for this, but I'm going to take the risk anyway.'

'What do you mean?' said Ivy, who was becoming increasingly curious.

'I don't know about you, but I had some really dud past lives and my current one, back in TWAWKI, isn't much better.'

'Right,' said Ivy, trying to work out where all this was leading.

'In fact, I really hate my life in TWAWKI. So things have got to change and I think that this is the place where I can make that happen.'

'So what are you thinking of?'

'Well, for a start – if I could get my own house, like you have.'

'Yeah, that would be good.'

This was extraordinary. I'd never heard Edith talking like this before. Was this how she really felt? If it was, she'd done a very good job of keeping her feelings to herself. That was for sure.

'Now, the fact you've done it means that you must know how to....'

'...work the system?' suggested Ivy.

'Exactly. And it seems that it might not be that hard. There's no police here, the head teacher's not much older than either of us. Who's really in charge?'

'Sure.'

'But that would be just the beginning.'

'The beginning of what?' asked Ivy.

'Taking over this island. That's what.'

I was so taken aback by this that my head bumped against the window sill.

'What was that?' said Ivy.

'Oh, nothing,' said Edith and then continued. 'I'm only saying this to you because you are the only person that I've met so far who would be brave enough and strong enough to do it.'

'Thank you,' said Ivy, obviously flattered by this remark. 'And what would you do if you took over the island?'

'I'd put an end to school for a start. We could – if you were to join me – use people in the way that Mr Subaltern has been accused of using them.'

'To work for us, you mean?'

'Exactly. We could build a whole little kingdom for ourselves here and have our own palace.'

'What, like the Venetian one?'

'Yes, we could take it over and develop it. And we could call it Pandemonium.'

'Isn't that what the devil called his?'

'Yeah, maybe. Anyway, are you in – or are you out?'

I took a quick peek to check that this really was Edith. It was, and either she was for real or she was playing some elaborate trick to get Ivy to talk.

'I'm in. In fact, I've already started paving the way,' said Ivy, boastfully.

'Oh, yes,' said Edith.

'There are various things that I've already got control of.'

'Oh, yes.'

'You've probably witnessed them in action. Your friend, Felix, for instance.'

'Oh, yes.'

'I did a couple of things to him.'

'What were they?'

'By making his life here so unpleasant, I thought I might get him on to my side.'

So it was Ivy who had been responsible for all this skulduggery. Why hadn't I realised that before? Why had I been so gullible and fallen for her charms? I zipped over to the front door and was just about to start hammering on it, when the dragonfly flew straight into my face and then hovered in front of me, fluttering its wings hypnotically. It was right. If I burst in now, everything that Edith was clearly trying to do would be ruined. So I took some deep breaths and returned to my original position and listened intently, as Ivy explained how she had gone up and changed my records in the log book. I then heard her tell Edith about the people who had been executed on Old Souls' Island in the Middle Ages and how she had used their spirits to possess George and Sanjay. I could tell that the ecstatic way in which Edith responded to all this was not because she was impressed with Ivy, but because she was thrilled to know that she was was right about this nasty sorceress.

'You weren't responsible for Felix's set to with Mr O'Flaherty?' she exclaimed.

'What do you think? Yes, of course, I was just taking advantage of his volatile nature.'

'And what about the collectors in the sanatorium?'

'Well, we don't want any second or third years coming back this year, do we? They'll be on the school's side. It'll be a much harder battle if we have them to contend with as well.'

The dragonfly started moving around urgently and I realised that this was my cue to depart. As I started to go however, I suddenly caught sight of a wolveraffe, which had begun to stir. As it looked up at me, I gave him a tentative little wave back and then cautiously tried stroking it. It didn't growl. Why would it? This thing had accompanied me on several walks, but not tonight. He dropped his head gently on to the ground, shut his eyes and appeared to go back to sleep.

I crept away slowly from him, so as not to cause any aggravation, until I'd got to the cliff path. Looking back, I could see that it had now got up, as had the rest of the pack. And suddenly, I panicked. All I could do was to run. And run I did. As I looked behind me, I could see that all of them were now coming after me, but not in the slow, measured way that they had before. They were racing now.

Although I had a head start on them, they were catching up by the second. The dragonfly, who had obviously got wise to this, led me off the path and into one of those tunnels, like the one I went through to get to school.

I ran as fast as I could through it, expecting to see some area of safety ahead of me. That was not to be though. In fact, it seemed to be leading to a dead end. I was running straight towards a rock face whilst these animals, that had turned from guardians to guard dogs, were almost on my heels. All I could do was to grab a branch from one of the trees, turn round and start trying to fend them off. But there were too many of them to prevent any one of them from biting into my arms, legs or torso.

That was just the beginning though. These things, because they were tall, could go for the neck. I watched with horror as the leader came straight at me and then with disbelief as it hit and bounced off a wall right in front of my nose. The trees either side of me had suddenly spread their branches out towards each other. The rest of the pack barked and howled, baring their teeth towards me, but they were unable to touch me. What was this wall that had suddenly appeared in front of me?

The bewildered pack continued their growling until they had run out of steam. Realising that I was on a useless mission, the leader turned away and the rest followed. As they got to the end of the tunnel and onto the path, they then broke out into a run and headed back to the cottage.

As I moved forward to peer through, the branches separated from each other and shrunk back to their original size. I looked up to see that the dragonfly had reappeared and I nodded several times as if to say 'thank you'. I was convinced that my friend must have had something to do with saving me. It did its usual somersault in response and then led me back to Mrs Higgins', where I crept in through the front door and was tucked up in bed in no time.

I had barely got to sleep though when I was awoken again. This time it was a knock on the door.

'Sorry, Felix,' whispered Edith as she opened the door. 'I just had to speak to you.'

'Sure,' I said cagily.

'I've just found out something really important, which will affect you in a big way. You know your friend Ivy?'

'Yeah.'

'Well, she's not who you think she is.'

'I know,' I said.

'How do you know?'

'I overheard your conversation.'

'Did you? How come?'

'Something told me that I should go down to the cottage.'

'What was that?'

'A friend of mine,' I said, cryptically.

'The dragonfly?'

'Yes.'

'So you heard what I got out of her?'

'Yes, I did. Boy, that was seriously devious though. The way you went about it.'

'Sometimes, it's the only way.'

'Did you see the wolveraffes?'

'Yes, we heard them from the cottage, howling away. Ivy thought that they were chasing one of those orkins, you know – the things that look like foxes.'

'I was the orkin,' I said.

'Oh, I see. Well as soon as they had returned to the cottage, they accompanied me back here. Anyway, I'd better get some shut eye. And so had you,' she said as she went out of the door.

'So now we know,' I said.

'Yes, now we know. The problem is…what do we do about it?'

'Right now, Ivy thinks that she has won. She knows that you're going to hate everything about this place and be happy to listen to anything that she suggests. You've just been locked up for a start. And she probably thinks that you're not going to be allowed to go back to school.'

'No, I suppose not.'

'So, you'll be putty in her hands, as long as you don't indicate to her that you've heard anything from me about her true intentions. So, you're the perfect person to go and live with her.'

'Go and live with her?'

'Yes. You can say that you haven't been allowed back to school or here, or at least that you've been told to find alternative accommodation. Once you're there, you can find out exactly how she works her powers.'

'Why don't we just tell the guides?'

'We need to find out much more about her before they get involved. The guides can't go and spy on her. And I wouldn't be able to either. I know too much. She's still trying to work out if she can trust me.'

'Ok. I'll go there,' I replied, as my head hit the pillow and drifted off into the land of dreams before I could say another word.

17. Hypnosis

The next day, I came downstairs to find that everyone was out. I helped myself to some breakfast and then headed off to Ivy's. As I arrived at the cottage, the wolveraffes sat up and looked at me. I approached cautiously, but they didn't appear to be particularly bothered by my arrival and let me pass without a fuss. I knocked on the door.

'Hey, Felix. What's going down?'

'I've been chucked out.'

'Of school. I heard.'

'And Mrs Higgins'. She doesn't want me there anymore,' I said, pointing to the bag that I'd slung over my shoulder.

'Great. You're staying with me then.'

'Can I? Thanks.'

'Come on in. I'll take you to your room.'

We went upstairs and she showed me the spare room.

'This feels just like home. It's got the same view as my room at Mrs Higgins' place.'

'Great. Only difference is that here you can say exactly what you want, whenever you wanna say it. But there you probably have to keep your lip buttoned.'

'Yes and there's **so** many things I want to say.'

'Feel free. It's Liberty Hall here.'

'Do you remember the first time I saw you, I wanted someone to take Jermaine and me back to TWAWKI.'

'Yes.'

'Well, I feel the opposite now. I hate every inch of this island – apart from here, of course. So much so that I don't want to leave until I've taken my revenge on it.'

'A lot of people feel like that. Including your friend Edith.'

'Really?'

'Has she not told you about our conversation?'

'No, we fell out. So we don't talk much at the moment,' I said, wondering whether I was being convincing enough. She did appear to be believing me though.

The sound of the front door slamming downstairs drew this conversation to an end.

'Oh, hang on. That's Jo going out. I need to speak to him…Anyway, you're safe here. That's the main thing. Just don't touch those Janus-facers,' she said as she left me to unpack. 'Not until you've got to know them.'

'Oh, I won't. Don't you worry,' I shouted back to her and then hovered by the doorway, listening intently to what was going on. The front door slammed again, which I thought must mean that Ivy had gone out to speak to Jo. So I crept down the stairs and crouched beneath the window that I had eavesdropped through before. Only this time, I was on the other side, of course.

'Ok, so here's the thing, Jo,' I could hear Ivy saying. 'Find out who her friends are and what she's said about me to them – in fact, anything you can.'

'Leave it to me.'

'Awesome. I'll see you this evening. Hopefully you'll have got some leads by then. So you can report back on your return.'

'What about Felix?' he whispered.

'Don't worry. He's cool. He'll be fine.'

I wasn't sure what she meant by that, but I wasn't going to hang around any longer for fear of being caught. So I crept back up to my room and waited for Ivy to go out.

'I'm off out now, Felix. See you for sups this evening,' Ivy called out from downstairs some minutes later.

'Thanks, Ivy. You've saved my life.'

'Don't even think about it.'

The front door slammed yet again and I took this as my opportunity to check out her book collection. I scoured the shelves but saw nothing particularly remarkable. Or at least unusual. Some great works of fiction sat side by side with each other, from Charles Dickens to J.R.R. Tolkien, but there was nothing out of the ordinary – at least at first glance. However, when I looked to see which Dickens novels Ivy had got, I noticed that most of them were hard back copies with loose covers.

The jacket for *Great Expectations* looked like it was too big for the book that was inside it though. So I pulled it out to discover that it had a blank cover and that all its contents inside had been handwritten, not printed. The title on the first page was *Magic and Ritual on Old Souls' Island*.

I quickly skimmed through the pages. There was a chapter on *Hypnotism* and another one on how to avoid it. That looked interesting. It said that in Rudyard Kipling's *Kim*, the main character prevents himself from falling under someone's spell by going through his ten times table in his head whilst someone else was trying to make him fall into a trance. What else was there? A chapter on *Sleeping Potions* and a picture of the plant, Somnicibus, that you could make one from. It looked like a flowering plant with all its colours reversed. The stem was bright yellow and the petals were light green.

Instructions: Crush up the petals, put into a cup, pour on hot water and then decant into another drinking vessel through a strainer.

Just like making a cup of tea with tea leaves. And then there was a chapter on *Calling up the Spirits*. I would have to leave that until another time though. Someone was approaching.

The door opened and Jo came in.

'Hi, man. How ya doin'? You've had a bit of a weird, freaky time out there, apparently.'

'Yeah, I have but I'm safe now.'

'Safe as you can ever be, man. It's really cool here.'

'Is it?' I said, seeing if I could get anything negative out of him.

'Yeah, man. Ivy's so cool and easy going.'

'She doesn't get you to do things for her or anything?' I asked.

'What like?'

'Well, I mean, it's her house. So surely you've got to pay for your keep in some way. You can't do that with money. So I thought that maybe you'd...or I'd...have to do some chores for her. Her dirty work.'

'Yeah. I do some washing up sometimes, but I really like that. It makes feel at one with myself.'

'No, I didn't mean that. I mean...you know.'

'No, I don't, man,' said Jo, slightly irritably.

'Well, for instance, say she didn't like someone, maybe she might get you or I to do something spiteful on her behalf...'

140

'Oh, no. You've got the wrong idea. She's really laid back. She just wants to help people, that's all.'

'Really?' I probed, trying to coax him even more to dish some dirt.

'Yes, really! You'll be fine here. Everything's safe here.'

Everything was not safe. Everything was evil. How could he possibly say that. I felt the impulse to grab him by the collar and 'tell him like it is'. But…**No**, I didn't behave like that anymore. Other tactics needed to be employed.

I couldn't work out whether this guy was either a very good actor or completely oblivious as to what was going on around him, or – and this was more likely – whether he'd been trapped by one of Ivy's spells.

'Anyways, I'm off out again. I'll be in and out.'

'Do you think that I can take one of these books up to my room?'

'Sure, man. That's what they're there for. Reading! That *Lord of The Rings* is really far out, man.'

'Yeah. I know. I've read it.'

'Yeah. So have I.'

'What, while you've been here?'

'Oh, yeah.'

'What about the Dickens?'

'No, I don't like anything Victorian, man. Not since I spent some time in that classroom.'

'Yeah, I know where you're coming from. Even so, I might try reading *Oliver Twist*, I think.'

I took the book off the shelf and went up to my room. It was a relief to get lost in someone else's world and to find out that life can be even worse for some people than it currently was for me.

Several hours later, Ivy came back and called up to me to come down.

'Hi, Felix. We're going to eat in a minute. Jo's cooked some really wicked Trailcon and Haloom thing, haven't you?'

'Yeah, man. You're going to love this.'

'But before we have sups here, we always play a game, don't we, Jo?'

'Yeah, it's great, man.'

'It's just one of those silly things that we've taken to doing. Anyway, I'll start. If you two sit on those chairs and, just to make it all really atmospheric, I'm going to turn the lights off. So all you can see is the log fire. Now really concentrate and look at that flame. Watch it move. Imagine that you are inside it, flickering away. Keep your eyes on it all the time.'

Her voice became increasingly soft and mesmeric. This was exactly what I had been expecting. Kim had done his ten times table. I could go one better than that. I tried to remember that algebraic equation that Jermaine had set me that day at school, constantly staring at the flame, so as not to raise suspicion.

'Now, you are losing sense of who you think you are.'

She was almost whispering to us by this point. All the while, I was trying to solve $x^2 + 9 = y^2$.

'In fact, you no longer are who you think you are. You've become neutral. You will do as I tell you. Jo, put your hands in the air and say "I'm an idiot" five times!'

He did so without any hint of embarrassment.

'Felix, come and kiss my hand.'

This was hardly difficult. So I did exactly as requested.

'Now, put your hand into that bowl of bobolate pudding.'

Again, nothing hard about that.

'And now dig a bit out and smother it all over your face and hair.'

This was pretty disgusting but easily achieved. My head just felt sticky and uncomfortable and I couldn't wait to get into the shower to wash it off. But I would just have to **wait**.

'And now, put your right index finger into the fire, Jo.'

142

I watched in amazement as Jo followed this instruction. He kept his finger there for over a minute and then started to withdraw it.

'Don't take it out until I say so.'

I could see that his finger was beginning to scald.

'OK. You may remove it now.'

Jo did so, but without any fuss. He must have been totally under her spell.

'Now, you! Felix.'

I placed my finger at the top of the flame and breathed in and out as deeply as possible. This was unbearable. I did still have the equation to work out, of course. Maybe that would distract me from the excruciating pain. If $x^2 + 9 = y^2$ and the unknowns were both positive integers, what were the values of x and y? If x was 2, then x^2 would be 4 and y^2 would be 4 + 9, which equalled 13. No, that wasn't a perfect square. What about if x were 4, then y^2 would be 16 + 9 which equalled 25. Now that was a perfect square and y would be the square root of it – 5.

'Alright. Take it out. Get a glass of water for Felix, Jo. His skin's burnt.'

I had passed the test without being hypnotised. So Jermaine's equation, which had frustrated me so much at school that day, had turned out to be a life saver.

Although I was in enormous pain over supper, I was also so relieved not to have fallen for Ivy's powers that the one balanced out the other. Almost! The pie was delicious though. Ivy had not been deceiving me on that score. As we finished up, Ivy laid bare her plans for the rest of the evening and the following day.

'After supper, guys, we're going to take the boat to the caves. I have a little mission that needs to be accomplished. Now, from the intel that Jo got on Edith, it looks like she isn't really the person she was making herself out to be the other day. So we need to get a couple of girls from her class to do some probing. Who are her best friends, Jo?'

'Felix and Jermaine.'

'Girls, stupid!'

'Oh, Jasmin and Jade.'

'Right, does she really trust them?' said Ivy, starting to get impatient.

'Yes.'

'In that case, we can get them to find out if she was telling the truth or not.'

'How do we do that, Ivy?' asked Jo.

'By getting some of **our** friends to infiltrate their very beings. That's how,' said Ivy, who then turned to look at me. 'Felix!'

'Yes.'

'Are you any good at rowing?'

'Yes.'

'Well, let's go then.'

18. Spirits and Potions

The moons were bright enough for us to scramble down the path to the beach, where Ivy's boat was moored. Once Ivy and Jo were in, I rolled my trousers up, pushed the dinghy further out into the water, climbed over the side, sat down, got my oars into position and started to row.

'Which way?'

'East. Keep going until I tell you.'

'Stop!' she shouted after about ten minutes. 'Now just head into that cave.'

I managed to row the dinghy into the sand and then jumped out, catching the rope that Jo had thrown me and securing it to a hook in one of the rocks.

'Take these candles,' said Ivy. 'You've got matches, haven't you?'

145

'Yeah.'

The cave interior was dark and damp, just like any other cave really. Ivy placed the candles in a circle large enough for us to stand in and then went round lighting them. She then began to chant as she lit each one.

'Give light unto these poor, forgotten souls. Let them now be remembered and cherished and loved. We come here in peace, only to acknowledge you.'

As she said this, I could suddenly feel the presence of something standing right next to me. I couldn't see anything but I could feel that there was someone who was very disturbed standing beside me. Then directly opposite, another one could be felt. This continued until eventually I counted a total of five spirits that had joined us. There was no let up in that energy as Ivy spoke softly to them.

'I need your help again, my friends. But this is a more subtle task than that of your last assignments. Instead of drawing upon your anger, this time I need you to be devious. Anyone who feels unqualified, I would ask you to step down.'

The energy that had so strongly vibrated opposite me was no longer there. I could almost see another two drift away, but the one next to me was as vibrant as ever.

'Good. We have two left. That's all we need. Your 'inhabitees' – the people who you will inhabit – are Jasmin and Jade. Understood!'

There was a movement in the air from both of them.

'Your task is to find out from Edith what her intentions **really** are. Does she want to work with me or is she deceiving me? In other words, find out what she honestly thinks of me. Tomorrow night, I want you to bring her to the cottage. If she is genuine, we'll all have supper together. If, however, this girl proves to be a traitor – kill her. I don't care how. Push her over the cliff and make it look like an accident. Understood!'

Another shift in the air.

146

'Good! I am most grateful,' she said, stepping out of the circle and beckoning to Jo and me to do the same. 'Boys! Pick up the candles!'

As I rowed Ivy and Jo back to the cove, I tried hard to make it look as though I was happy with what had just happened. My mind was racing though, trying to work out how I could possibly get a message to Edith. However, unless my dragonfly friend was around – which he wasn't, there was absolutely nothing that I could think of.

'I expect that you'll both want to get straight to bed,' said Ivy as she opened the front door.

'Oh, yes. Definitely,' answered Jo immediately.

'Yes, definitely,' I reiterated.

'Keep vigilant, guys!' she said to her long-necked friends and then locked the door and took away the key.

I went straight to my room, dropped onto my bed and tried to work out a plan. There was no way that I could get out of the house tonight to go and warn Edith. The front door was locked and the wolveraffes were on high alert. If Ivy and Jo were around all the next day, I was stumped unless I could...But overwhelmed by the uselessness of it all, I drifted off into a stupor. A few hours later though, I woke up with a start. Sleep! Of course! I could make up a sleeping potion and give it to Ivy and Jo during the day. I sneaked downstairs, pulled out the book of magic from the shelves and wrote down the recipe and the description of the Somnicibus plant. As I put the manual back, disguised in its *Great Expectations* cover, I felt like I was in some kind of story myself. But I wasn't. I really was here in this living nightmare. Hoping that my dreams might be a bit more pleasant, I headed back to bed.

The following morning, Ivy played another one of her 'games' with Jo and me. So this was how she kept control over Jo. She'd have to reboot the hypnosis in the morning and the evening to ensure that he never slipped out of it. Another algebraic equation was called for…and quickly…or perhaps I could just return to a dream that I'd once had. The one I had actually lived for real in another life – in which the peak of Everest was only a few feet away.

When it was my turn to put my finger in the fire, I imagined that my hands were frozen to the bone and that any kind of warmth was welcome even though this was burning me. It didn't matter whether I kept them in the fire or took them out. The pain would be just as bad from the frost bite as it would be from the burning.

'Alright, you can take it out, Felix,' said Ivy.

'Oh, thank you,' I said calmly.

Once the ritual was over, I asked Ivy if I could do some gardening.

'It's really just for something to do, apart from anything else. And I quite enjoy getting my hands dirty.'

'Sure. Are you any good?'

'Yeah, I do quite a lot on my grandpa's allotment.'

'Well, I guess I can just leave you to it then.'

I got down to some weeding to begin with, checking with Ivy first that what looked like weeds were weeds and not some precious plants. No sign of the Somnicibus though, at least not to begin with. Not until my friend the dragonfly magically appeared just at the moment that I was about to lose all hope. It hovered above me for a second and then slowly, so as not to make me look suspicious, led me down the path to a row of bushes. I took a quick look over my shoulder to check that neither Ivy or Jo were looking out of the window, as they had been intermittently, and scrambled through the thicket to see what was there: a whole clump of flowering plants, which looked identical to the ones in *Magic and Ritual on Old Souls' Island* – unmistakable because of their bright yellow stems. I quickly pulled a couple out of the ground and then returned to put them into my basket of weeds. Just in time, it would seem, as Ivy suddenly came out of the back door.

'Want some hot bobolate, Felix?

'In about half an hour, if that's OK.'

'Sure, I'll hang on until you've finished,' she said as she went back into the house.

There was no sign of either Ivy or Jo leaving the cottage that day. So there was no chance of getting away from the place to see Edith or at least to get a message to her. When it got dark, I went back into the house. I knew that the girls would be due to make their way down to the cottage shortly, so I had to get on with things.

'That's a great job that you've done out there,' said Ivy. 'I've been meaning to do it myself, but I just can't be bothered. And Jo's useless. He'd pick the flowers and leave all the weeds.'

'Like I nearly did.'

'Do you want that bobolate now?'

'Oh, yes. I'd love one. Do you?' I said, attempting to sound helpful.

'Yes. I'll make it.'

'No, don't worry. I will.'

'Thanks, Felix. I'm feeling a bit lazy today.'

'Jo!'

'Yes please, Felix.'

I went into the kitchen, pulled the plants out of my pocket and found a knife to chop the petals up with. I then put them into a cup, which I filled with hot water. Once it had all brewed, I poured it through a strainer into a mug and then tipped a bit of my preparation into Ivy's bobolate and some into Jo's. I then hid the rest of it at the back of one of the cupboards, in case I needed it later.

'Oh, thanks, Felix. You really are a proper man about the house,' she said as she took the mug away from me. 'Um,

Lovely. Nice mug of bobolate, houseboy! What have you put in it?'

'Just the usual stuff,' I said, surprising even myself with how innocent I'd managed to sound.

'Oh, it tastes a bit different. That's all. It's probably just the way you make it.'

'Yes, probably. Oh, god. I haven't put the garden tools away.'

'Don't worry. You can do that tomorrow…'

'No, I'll do it now if that's all right.'

'I said – you can do it tomorrow,' repeated Ivy firmly, suspicious now that I may not be sufficiently hypnotised.

'Sorry, I just wanted to do the right thing,' I said, sensing what she might be thinking.

'Well, the right thing is to…Oh, god! I suddenly feel a bit tired. And Jasmin and Jade are coming over later, aren't they?'

'Yes, I think they are.'

'Oh, well. I'll probably…'

But with that, she was out for the count.

'Hey, man. What did you put in this bobolate? I'm out of it,' said Jo, as he too slumped back in his armchair and fell asleep.

How long this stuff lasted I didn't know, but I had to act quickly. I went out of the front door and walked casually past the wolveraffes, who looked up disinterestedly at me. My body was shaking nervously, but I managed to keep my composure enough to disguise this.

As I got to the cliff path, I could see Edith walking down towards the cottage with Jasmin and Jade. I should have timed this better. If I ran up to them, I could probably prevent them from carrying out Ivy's orders but that would get the wolveraffes going. I couldn't risk that after what happened last time. So I had to continue, for the moment, to just walk slowly towards them.

Suddenly an argument broke out between the girls. This was definitely the beginning of the end. So there was nothing for it. I had to run up to them. The wolveraffes sussed this from half a mile away and came chasing up towards us. I pulled Edith away from the other two and shouted: 'Run!' And run they did.

'We have to get down to the cove,' I shouted.

'You grab the boy,' called out Jasmin to Jade, 'and I'll deal with Little Miss Turncoat here.'

'But, I'm not a turncoat. I didn't know which side you were on. I thought you both were goody-two-shoes. Anyway, if we don't stop fighting and shift our backsides, those wolveraffes will get us all. The reason why their necks are so long is so that they can bite into our jugulars.'

'What are they?' said Jade.

'These things,' said Edith, pointing to her neck. 'They'll kill you in other words.'

'Let's get down to the cove and into the boat. It's our only hope,' I shouted.

The girls, despite the fact that they were possessed, were too scared not to do as I suggested. They ran down the path with the wolveraffes slipping and sliding behind them.

'Jump in! Quickly!' I shouted.

As the girls were all getting themselves seated, I pushed the boat out. The wolveraffes were obviously terrified of the water as they didn't get a paw wet. However, they still were able to reach my legs and were tearing my trousers off me and biting into my flesh, which prevented me from being able to make any progress with my pushing. I was done for and could feel myself getting weaker.

'You've got to get to the cave and...'

Suddenly the wolveraffes released their grip from my legs. Edith, cottoning on to how much they hated salt water, had started to splash them. I jumped into the boat, grabbed the oars and started rowing. The wolveraffes continued to howl.

Despite the pain I was in, the adrenalin in my system gave me the strength to keep going until we had arrived at the cave. I jumped out, tied the boat up and grabbed the candles and matches.

'Come into the cave. I want to show you something,' I said to them.

'Are you kidding?' said Jasmin.

'No. Come in,' I said, arranging and lighting the candles as before. I had no idea what I was doing but I had to do something. 'Please, stand in the circle with me.'

Once we were all positioned, I started to chant.

'Give light unto these poor, forgotten souls. Let them be remembered and cherished and loved. We come here in peace, only to acknowledge you. We are grateful for all you have done for us. It's time to go home now though. Time to go home. Time to go home. Time to go home.'

Suddenly, Jasmin and Jade looked at Edith and me in disbelief.

'Where are we?' said Jade.

'What are we doing here?' said Jasmin.

'Just saying goodbye to some **old** friends,' I replied.

'Oh. Can we go back now?'

'Yes, we can.'

When we got back to the cove, the wolveraffes were still waiting at the water's edge, looking just as vicious as they had done before. I rowed the boat up to them and then quickly turned it around and headed back out to sea, round the headland and into the next-door cove.

'Can you swim?' I said to the girls.

'Yes,' they all replied in unison.

'Well, swim back to the beach that we've just come from. I'll distract them in the other cove.'

All three girls jumped out of the boat and did as I suggested. In the meantime, I kept rowing the boat towards the next beach. The wolveraffes had by this time climbed up to the top of the cliff and were beginning to come down the path on the other side and head in my direction. I pulled the front part of the boat onto the sand and then jumped back in again. The wolveraffes surrounded the boat's bow, but I was sitting right at the other end.

As their barking and howling reached fever pitch, one of the wolveraffes took the initiative and jumped into the dinghy and the others followed immediately afterwards. Almost simultaneously, I threw myself overboard into the water and then pulled the boat out to sea. The wolveraffes were now both terrified and frightened, howling and biting at my hands. As they got more confident, they stuck their necks out and grabbed the part of my arm that was above the water with their teeth. I used my other hand to splash them until eventually they let go, allowing me to swim round to the front of the boat and grab the rope, which I then tied to a rock. 'Good!' I thought. They'd be stuck there until the tide had gone back out and the boat was on dry land again.

I then swam back into the other cove, where Edith was waiting for me. She told me that Jade and Jasmin had gone back home – after they'd received a full explanation – and then helped me up to the cliff path. As we made our way back to the cottage, the wolveraffes' howls became fainter and fainter.

19. Return Journey

By the time we opened the front door, Ivy and Jo were just coming to.

'Hi, Ivy. Thanks for inviting me,' said Edith cheerfully.

'Oh, hi Edith. I didn't think that you'd make it.'

'Oh, why would that have been?'

'Just didn't. Where's Jasmin and Jade?'

'They went home.'

'Oh, did they?...Sorry, I'm really dozy.'

'Make her a boffee, Felix,' said Edith.

'OK. Do you want one, Jo?'

'Yeah, man. I could really do with one.'

I went into the kitchen, reached into the cupboard for my potion and made two steaming cups of boffee, one 'with' and one 'without'.

'How's that? Feeling better,' said Edith, as Ivy knocked back the contents of her cup.

'Yes, I think I…'

And with that, she was off again.

'How about you, Jo?' I asked.

'Yeah, I'm fine. Much better. Ta, man.'

'So you should be. You didn't have any…'

'Any what, man?'

'Don't worry. Forget about that? Do you fancy playing a game?'

I knew that I had to un-hypnotise him and I had to do it now. But how?

'Hang on,' I said, realising exactly where I could find out. 'That *Great Expectations* book's got a really good one in.'

'I suppose it would with a name like that.'

I pulled the book in question off the shelf and thumbed through it until I got to the chapter on hypnosis.

'Here we go. Let's turn out the lights. Now, Jo, look into the fire. The fire is your friend. Think of nothing else and look at nothing else but the flames. They are your friends. At least, you think they are your friends. Let's go and touch them and see if they still are.'

Jo went and stood by the fire uncertainly.

'Go on. Touch them.'

He reached out his hand and then quickly took them away again.

'I said touch them!'

'I can't.'

'Try!'

'Ok, man. I'll try.'

He put his finger in quickly, but then immediately withdrew it.

'Ow. That hurts, man.'

'Good.'

155

'What do you mean…**Good**?'

'I mean…**Good**. Welcome back to the real world, where you can make your own decisions instead of following someone else's orders.'

'You mean…**hers**?' he said, pointing at Ivy.

'Now, we have to work fast,' Edith intervened. 'You're a collector, aren't you, Jo?'

'Yes. Sure am.'

'I can't explain this all now, but Ivy must get home to her parents.'

'Must she?'

'Yes, it's a matter of urgency. She's been missing back in TWAWKI for over a year now and they've almost given up hope. They may have been hopeless as parents, but they are really suffering now and they would do anything to have her back.'

'Really?' I said.

'Yes, really. What's the old traffic like between here and TWAWKI at the moment, Jo?'

'Should be fine. The other collectors are all ill.'

'Do you think you could do it?' said Edith.

'What, now?'

'Yes, while she's asleep. She won't go otherwise.'

'Well, I'm not sure that she'll be too happy about that.'

'If you don't take her, there are going to be two people who are going to be a darn sight unhappier,' said Edith. 'And if you do, she'll change not just her parents' lives but her own one as well. For the first time in her life, she'll be loved and that's a pretty good start. She may cause trouble back in TWAWKI, but that would be absolutely miniscule in comparison with what she could do if she stays here. She can use her powers here, but she can't back in TWAWKI. Apparently, she was never trained up as a Sagacitor as they couldn't find out who she was in a previous life. That's why they stuck her out here in this cottage.

156

They didn't know what to do with her and she was causing far too much trouble in the palace'

'But if she gets taken home, won't she just come back again?' I said. 'If she wakes up before six in the morning, that is.'

'No, she won't. She can't,' said Jo. 'One of the reasons she didn't go back is because she isn't a collector. She's got all these other powers or at least she knows how to use them, but the school refused to give her the ability to move freely from one dimension to another. If she wants to come back, she would have to be collected…OK, I'll do it.'

Edith and I did a silent hurrah so as not to wake Ivy.

'Well there's no time like…'

'Now,' said Jo, as he pulled out his planium tops and set them spinning on the floor. He then picked up Ivy from the chair, held her in his arms and went into deep concentration.

'See you in five, guys!'

And he was off. When he reappeared five minutes later, Edith and I were able to give a fully vocalised cheer.

'How was that, Jo?' asked Edith.

'Yeah, perfect. She's sound asleep in her own bed. Just as I left, I made enough noise to wake her parents up, who got up and went to check her room seconds after I was out of sight.'

'Good work, Jo,' said Edith. 'Do you think that you can take Felix back as well? He needs a fresh start.'

'And Jermaine?' I added.

'If you like, although we better get on with it. The second years are coming back tomorrow.'

'Are they?'

'Yes. All the collectors have had some kind of miracle recovery apparently.'

'That's interesting,' said Edith, working this out.

'Yes. Adrian's already back in business. I just met him en route. The rest of them are going to do a full-on day tomorrow.

There's a lot of very restless second years, sitting up in bed twiddling their thumbs, waiting to be picked up.'

'Why do people keep coming back? Surely, you'll have done everything you need to after the first year's over.'

'Oh, no. That's just the beginning. As you get older, you're allowed to go to some of the other islands.'

'What happens there?'

'Well, on certain islands, some people actually become one of their previous lives, twenty-four hours a day.'

'Wow!'

'And properly too. They morph into that person, just like you would have done in the Warriors Room, and then they stay as that person. They can then teach you how they used their powers as Sagacitors on TWAWKI. There's one island that's full of musicians. I can't wait to go there. My greatest ambition is to meet Jimi Hendrix.'

'Oh, wow. Is he there? We're going to have to come back. He's my favourite, man.'

'Yeah, you'll come back all right,' said Edith. 'You just need to have a fresh start, Felix, that's all.'

'Yes, I'll come back again next year,' I said. 'By then, everyone will know what really happened.'

'We better get going for now, though. Our work is done here.'

'OK. When do you want to go?' asked Jo.

'In about half an hour. Just got to say goodbye to Mrs Higgins.'

We walked up the hill to Mrs Higgins' and told her all about everything that had happened to us. She listened intently as she disinfected my wounds and then dressed them. When Jermaine came downstairs, we told him what the plan was.

'Oh my days. So we are going back after all. I was just beginning to enjoy it here. But it wouldn't be the same without my best mate.'

'Would you mind telling the head teacher what has happened, Mrs Higgins?'

'I will. Don't you worry, I'll explain everything. I knew that there was something strange about that girl the moment I set eyes on her.'

'Sorry to say goodbye, Mrs Higgins.'

'So am I. I see people come and go, year in and year out. So I should be used to this by now. But I'm not. And not with you two. I'm going to admit to having a real soft spot for you boys. Just when I thought we were all nice and settled. You will come back, won't you. I'm going to miss you...'

She was unable to hold back the tears any longer and we both gave her a hug.

'Bye, Edith. See you at school, tomorrow,' I said, suddenly realising afterwards that it wouldn't be quite like that for her. 'Or rather...'

'...In a year's time,' she said.

'Yeah. In a year's time. Cheerybye.'

Jo and I went out onto the cliff top, from where I could just see that Stonehenge was back to its normal colour. We then prepared ourselves for the journey home. Just as I was about to close my eyes though, I was distracted by my friend, the dragonfly, who had landed on my shoulder.

'Oh, you've come to say goodbye. I'll miss you, but I'm coming back.'

It fluttered its wings, but made no attempt to move.

'You can't come with me. I'm going back to TWAWKI,' I explained.

'Who you talking to, man?' said Jo, as he set the tops in motion.

'I was just saying to my friend, the dragonfly, that he can't come with me. But he won't budge.'

'Don't worry about insects, man.'

'I think he might be a bit more than that.'

'Doesn't matter,' said Jo, gathering up the tops. 'It's you that's important. Right, off we go!'

As with the last time, I felt myself being pulled in both directions until, that is, I passed out. The next thing I knew was that I was back in my bedroom at Trevelyan Tower, very quietly saying my goodbyes to Jo. After he'd gone, I looked at my watch. Thirteen minutes past twelve. That was alright. I shouldn't be too sleepy the next day at school after all. What about the dragonfly though? I put my hand into my jacket pocket and fished out what felt like a piece of jewellery. My insect friend had turned to stone, even though its multi-coloured scales were glittering as much as they ever had done. I held him in my hand and just looked at him. But then, there it was again. That presence that I'd felt in my room just before I'd set off for Old Souls'.

I wrapped the dragonfly up in a tissue and hid it away in a drawer and got ready for bed. As I was putting on my pyjamas, I suddenly heard a noise outside the door and poked my head round to see what it was. My dad was sitting on the sofa with his head in his hands.

'Dad,' I said, giving him a bit of a nudge.

'Yes,' muttered Dad. 'Sorry, Son. Did I wake you?'

'No, I was still up.' If only he knew!

'I didn't want to disturb you.'

'Well, you didn't.'

'It's your grandpa.'

'What do you mean?'

'He pressed his alarm button and I went down to see him. I was hoping you wouldn't hear.'

'Oh, yes. I did hear you go out,' I said, remembering.

'Well, it happened shortly after that. Just as I went into the flat.'

'What happened?'

'He was very peaceful, Son. I would have come and told you but I didn't want to wake you.'

'Do you mean he's…'

'Yes, Son.'

'Oh, no. Oh, I knew this was going to happen.'

'Yes, so did he.'

We both stood looking at the floor for some considerable time, until I broke the silence.

'What time did he die?'

'I did look at my watch as it happens. Sometimes people ask you these things. 23.45.'

'Oh.'

'About 25 minutes ago. I left the ambulance crew to sort everything out.'

Again, we were lost for words.

'Did Grandpa like dragonflies?' I said after a while.

'What are you on about, Son?'

'Oh, nothing.'

'I think he did, now you mention it. Anyways, you get yourself to bed.'

'I will.'

'What's happened to your hand, Son?'

'Got bitten by a dog.'

'Oh, I didn't notice that before. You kept that hidden.'

'It's alright. It's all been disinfected properly.'

'Where is this dog now? Do you know who's it was?'

'Yes. It's been dealt with, Dad. I think it's learnt its lesson.'

'Oh alright, Son. Goodnight.'

'Goodnight, Dad.'

'Goodnight, Son. We'll get through this.'

'Yeah, Dad. We will.'

THE END